"Lauren? It [...] *he said with a soft lilt of anticipation.*

Her stomach clenched. The archdeceiver himself! If he thought she was about to rush in and beg for more, he could think again.

"Yes?" she queried, her mind suddenly cold and clear.

"I found your note. It was a great night for me, too."

"I'm glad it was mutual," she replied silkily, waiting for the perfect line to turn the knife.

He laughed. "Couldn't be more so. When do you think you'll finish work tonight?"

"Oh, I don't know. What do you want, Michael?" That was a good question. Let him beg!

"I'll be with you again as soon as you're free."

She deliberately heaved a sigh. "Look, Michael, it was a great night. A really great night. Let's leave it at that, shall we?"

Silence. "Come again?" He sounded puzzled, disbelieving.

Lauren went in for the kill. "Well, the fact of the matter is that I don't go in for repeat performances. Why spoil a perfect memory?"

EMMA DARCY nearly became an actress, until her fiancé declared he preferred to attend the theater with her. She became a wife and mother. Later she took up oil painting—unsuccessfully, she remarks. Then she tried architecture, designing the family home in New South Wales, Australia. Next came romance writing— "the hardest and most challenging of all the activities," she confesses.

Books by Emma Darcy

EMMA DARCY

The Father of Her Child

Harlequin Books

TORONTO • NEW YORK • LONDON
AMSTERDAM • PARIS • SYDNEY • HAMBURG
STOCKHOLM • ATHENS • TOKYO • MILAN
MADRID • WARSAW • BUDAPEST • AUCKLAND

For Sue Curran, my editor,
in warm appreciation of her sharing and caring

ISBN 0-373-11833-3

THE FATHER OF HER CHILD

First North American Publication 1996.

Copyright © 1996 by Emma Darcy.

CHAPTER ONE

"LAUREN says..."

Michael Timberlane's jaw clenched. His friend and client, Evan Daniel, continued talking, blithely ignorant of the effect of those two explosively evocative words...*Lauren says*. Michael didn't hear anything else. His mind filled with brooding resentment.

He couldn't count the number of times his ex-wife had thrown those words at him as though Lauren Magee was the font of all knowledge and wisdom on how a marriage should work. *Lauren says, Lauren says*...a long litany of feminist claptrap that had given Roxanne the encouragement to indulge herself in single-minded selfishness. Any sense of give and take had flown right out the door under Lauren Magee's influence.

It was a black day when that woman had accepted the position as publicist at the publishing house where Roxanne worked in marketing. Why the Sydney branch of Global Publications had to import a career woman from Melbourne to head its publicity department was beyond Michael's comprehension, but the word in the industry was that Lauren Magee was a fireball. She obviously didn't mind whom she scorched, either.

Michael grudgingly conceded he had not been averse to the idea of divorce by the time Roxanne decided it was what she wanted. His ideal of a true partnership within a love relationship had been comprehensively whittled away. Nevertheless, Evan's inadvertent reminder of the interfering judgments by a woman who didn't even know him stirred a vengeful wish to turn Lauren Magee and her insidious list of women's rights upside down and inside out.

Would that he could!

It was undoubtedly a waste of energy even thinking about it. The woman had to be a man hater with a brick-wall temperament, totally closed to logic or reason. She would probably have Evan's balls for breakfast if he stepped out of line on this promotional tour she had organised for him. A male author who liked an alcoholic lunch would not be her cup of tea at all.

Michael unclenched his jaw, relaxed his facial muscles and dutifully tuned back into Evan's flow of excitement over his jam-packed schedule of interviews with the media. Global Publications, via Lauren Magee, was certainly doing him proud in their efforts to launch his new historical novel on the Australian reading public. Michael hoped it would sell well, not only for his friend's sake, but also for his own satisfaction as Evan's literary agent.

He silently congratulated himself on getting Evan an extremely good deal for the book, though he would have privately preferred the highest bidder to have been any other publishing house than Global Publications. But business was business. The best interests of all the authors on his list had to be served. That was one of the principles by which he'd gained his reputation as an agent whose judgment could be trusted.

He knew books. He knew what they were worth and where their market was. Evan Daniel's sweeping saga of early colonial days in the convict settlement of New South Wales was a rattling good story and had the elements for solid, commercial success. All it needed was the right push to bring it to public attention.

"I need your help, Michael."

Evan's excitement seemed to have faded into a sudden fit of anxiety. Michael raised his eyebrows, inviting elaboration on whatever problem was troubling his friend. This had to be the underlying reason for his visit this morning. It was a long drive from Evan's home at Leura in the Blue Mountains to Michael's apartment-cum-office at Milson's Point in the very heart of Sydney. Enthusing over his promotional tour hardly constituted a strong enough motive to bring him here.

All the signs of inner agitation were evident. Evan shifted his somewhat roly-poly body uncomfortably. He tugged at the frizzy brown curls above his ears, pulling them out into tufts. With his round face and big, dark, soulful eyes, Evan frequently reminded Michael of a cuddly koala bear. Despite his rotund shape, women were attracted to him.

There was something very appealing about Evan. His bright and benevolent personality reached out to people.

"Could you take the time off to come with me on the tour to Melbourne and Brisbane?" he finally blurted out.

"You don't need me to hold your hand, Evan. You'll do fine. Your natural enthusiasm about your book..."

"It's not that. I'm not scared of the interviews," came the hasty assurance. His ensuing grimace held both apology and an appeal for understanding. "It's Tasha. She's going to be rabidly jealous of Lauren the moment she lays eyes on her."

Michael was astounded. "Lauren Magee?"

"You know how gorgeous she is. And I'll be staying in the same hotels with her."

"Lauren Magee...gorgeous?" Michael couldn't believe it. In his mind's eye Lauren Magee was a sexless martinet, as thin as a matchstick with every bit of feminine sweetness squeezed out of her.

Evan looked puzzled. "Haven't you met her?"

It would be pistols at dawn if he did, Michael thought darkly. "I can't say I've had the pleasure," he drawled with deliberate carelessness.

"I thought you knew everyone in the publishing industry."

Evan's surprise was comical. Michael had to smile. "The publishers and the commissioning editors, yes. I haven't met every single person on their staffs."

"But Lauren ... Oh, well, you can meet her at the party tonight. I'll introduce you. Then you'll see why I need you to come with me on the tour. I know it's asking a big favour, Michael, but..."

"I won't be there tonight," Michael stated flatly.

It was Global's launching party for all its new books for the coming year. Roxanne would be swanning around with her second choice of husband, who was, Michael thought cynically, quite perfect for her. Her preening didn't bother him, but she made such a pointed show of it in front of him he felt sorry for the other guy. It was distasteful. Such comparisons always were.

Michael prided himself on being civilised. Most of the time he was. Very civilised. Extremely civilised. The combination of Roxanne on parade, trying in her perverse vanity to make a fool of him, plus Lauren Magee on the sidelines with her feminist cant, just happened to bring out the savage in him. It was not a feeling he liked.

Evan looked hurt. "I'm one of the speakers."

"I'm sorry, Evan, but you don't need me to applaud your speech."

"I do need you. Not for applause. If I could stand you between Tasha and Lauren, it would save me a power of trouble. Tasha wouldn't get any funny ideas with you around. It's perfectly obvious that any woman with two eyes in her head would go for you, not me."

That wasn't necessarily true, Michael thought. Superficially, he supposed, he fitted the tall, dark and handsome tag, but in a savage mood, he knew he could look more intimidating than attractive.

"And if you came on tour with me," Evan pressed, "Tasha would have no reason to get upset."

The impassioned plea tried Michael's patience. "Your marital problems are none of my business, Evan. If you can't assure your wife of your unbreakable fidelity, take her with you."

"You know Tasha is eight months pregnant," came the plaintive protest. "Can you see her manoeuvring into an economy-class seat on one of those small intercity planes? Not to mention her doctor's orders to rest and take care. We're not taking any chances with this baby. Not after two miscarriages."

Michael frowned. He had forgotten Tasha's delicate condition and the trouble she'd had in carrying a child to full term. Evan was right. It was stupid to take any risk. If it was his wife and baby Michael knew he'd be cocooning them in cotton wool.

His desire to have children had been frustrated by Roxanne's deceptions, and he wondered now if he'd ever get to be a father. Finding the right woman had to come first. He assured himself that at thirty-four, he was still in his prime and his choices in life were wide open. He was not restricted by time.

"Surely Tasha can trust you," he offered. "It's only for a few days."

Evan sighed. "Normally, yes, but she's in a very fragile mood, feeling all lumpy and undesirable. We've had to refrain from sex because... Well, I don't want to go into that." He flushed. "Anyhow, she's not going to be happy about me flying off with a woman as gorgeous and sexy-looking as Lauren Magee."

Lauren Magee sexy-looking? Michael shook his head incredulously. That was wrapping a wormy apple in a glossy skin.

The glum, discomforted face of his friend stirred sympathy. Evan and Tasha were going through a tough time. The successful launching of this book was important to them financially, so it couldn't be dropped, and Evan was quite likely to fumble the interviews and get smashed on double gins if he was upset.

"Please?" he begged. "There's no one else I can turn to. If you don't help me...." He rolled his eyes and gestured despairingly.

Michael's curiosity was piqued. "Do you like her, Evan?" he asked pertinently.

"Who? Lauren?" He looked innocent. "She's a lovely girl, but I'm a married man, Michael. I love my wife and I'm not about to stray." Hotly earnest.

"Does she like you?"

Uncomfortable shifting again. "Well, er, only in a friendly kind of way. I just don't want Tasha to misunderstand. If you're with me, everything will be all right."

A nasty little troublemaker, amusing herself by coming between husbands and wives, Michael thought with considerable venom. Not this time, Lauren Magee, he silently vowed. *Lovely girl*...huh! She might be gorgeous and sexy-looking, but she clearly had the sting of an asp, poisoning other people's relationships.

Michael decided it would give him immense satisfaction to do a bit of stinging of his own. Besides, Tasha deserved to have peace of mind during this difficult period. The strain of an advanced and possibly threatened pregnancy was more than enough for her and Evan to cope with. Protecting them from any capricious harm by Lauren Magee was the decent thing to do.

"Okay, Evan, I'll run interference for you," he said, a dangerous little smile lurking on his lips.

Relief burst over his friend's face. "At the party tonight? And the tour?"

"Yes. You can count on me for both."

And to hell with Roxanne and her ridiculous gloating with her new husband! He could stomach that if he had to for one evening. It was in a good cause. As for Lauren Magee, well, he was beginning to look forward to locking horns with her.

Evan surged out of his chair and reached over Michael's desk to grab his hand and shake it vigorously with both of his. "You're a true, true friend and I thank you from the bottom of my heart. It means I can relax and enjoy everything, and Tasha will, too. She's been looking forward to tonight's launching party. Wouldn't miss it for anything."

"Then I hope she'll have a happy evening."

Evan grinned. "Champagne on tap. I love free drinks."

"Don't forget you have to drive," Michael warned dryly.

"Uh-uh. We're staying in the city overnight. Taxis both ways."

"What hotel? I could pick you up. Best if we arrive together, don't you think?"

"Great!" Evan heaved a huge, contented sigh. "I won't forget this, Michael. Any time you want a favour, you've got it."

"I'll remember that. Do you have a list of the tour details with you...dates, times, flights, hotels?"

"Sure do. With all the telephone numbers for you to make your bookings."

Evan was probably right about no-one else being able to help him, Michael reflected a few minutes later. The cost of this safeguard venture would prohibit most people. Money meant nothing to him, never had, and Evan knew it. Real friendship did. All the wealth in the world couldn't buy that. If a couple of thousand dollars could prevent Tasha and Evan from being messed up by Lauren Magee, Michael was only too happy to supply the necessary.

That lady had a few things coming to her.

Michael figured he was just the man to deliver them.

He could feel the primitive savage stirring inside him, and this time he didn't try to suppress the feeling. He revelled in it. Being civilised could definitely be overrated. He had the taste of revenge in his mouth. It was sweet.

CHAPTER TWO

"COME on, Lauren," Graham Parker urged. "It's peak hour, remember? The traffic across the city is bound to be horrendous, and I want to make it to Rose Bay by six."

"I'm coming." The last page of the publicity flyer started rolling through the fax machine. Confident there'd be no problem with the transmission, Lauren turned to her desk, snatched up her handbag and flashed a smile at the head of the marketing department. "Ready to go."

Graham was in his mid-forties, solidly married to his wife, family and computer and nicely avuncular towards her. Lauren knew he read nothing personal into her asking him for a lift to the launching party. It was simply a convenience between two coworkers. She always felt in a comfort zone with Graham. It was a pleasant feeling.

"Snazzy belt," he commented appreciatively.

She grinned, pleased with the compliment. The belt was a recent purchase, featuring a large gold bow set on a wide, black, elasticised band. "Nothing like a good accessory to turn day wear into glitz."

He shook his head in bemusement as she joined him. "Do you turn your whole life into a time and motion study?"

"Have to with my job, Graham."

"I don't know how you can stand the pace. Always on the go. It would give me a coronary."

"I like it."

It filled her life. She needed that. She didn't like having too much time to dwell on the empty spaces. It was good to keep busy. Besides, she was doing what she did best, organising schedules, taking care of people, sorting them out, fitting everything and everyone into a workable and effective pattern. It seemed to Lauren she had been doing that as long as she could remember, having been the eldest child in a family of nine.

Once she had dreamed of having someone take care of her and do all the looking after. Big mistake. Her stomach clenched in recoil at the memory of the prison her ex-husband had made of their marriage. Never again, she vowed. Obsessive possessiveness had no place in Lauren's concept of love. It was both frightening and crushing.

As she rode the elevator to the ground floor with Graham, she consciously banished those shadows from her mind. These days she lived life on her own terms, and the party tonight should be fun. No responsibilities for her apart from chatting to a few authors, making them feel welcome and introducing them to other guests. Champagne was to flow freely and a band had been booked to provide dance music after the speeches. Lauren loved dancing.

She adjusted the new belt so the gold bow was set closer to her hip line. It looked brilliant on the bright violet of her ribbed knit sweater. She was really pleased with the overall effect, the wide black elastic accentuating the black of her skirt and tights and the bow picking up the gold trim on her black suede shoes.

She still had to do her hair. It was in a bit of a tangle from being loose all day. Lauren grinned to herself as she recalled her hairdresser calling it a wild animal. The copper-red hue did not come out of a bottle and the natural curls bounced from her scalp and rioted over her shoulders and halfway down her back.

Once she was in Graham's car she would pile up her unruly hair and clip on the black and gold earrings. That would certainly put the finishing touch to her cocktail-hour appearance.

Graham hustled her out of Global's office building to the car park, clearly anxious to be on his way. By Lauren's calculation, from where they were in Artarmon, the express route to the bridge and the Harbour Tunnel to the Eastern Suburbs cut the trip to Rose Bay to forty minutes at most, even through peak hour traffic. The party didn't start until six, and it was only just past five now.

"Why the hurry?" she asked. Accustomed to travelling to a tight schedule, Lauren disliked the waste of time involved in arriving anywhere too early.

"I want to check the display table before anyone arrives."

"I thought Roxanne was doing that."

She had told Lauren so this morning, pleased with the task of setting up a display of the new titles catalogue and the gift T-shirts.

"She tripped down the steps out there and sprained her ankle," Graham stated flatly.

Lauren rolled her eyes. Another drama in Roxanne's life to be endlessly recounted to every ear she could find!

"I don't know if she finished the job first," Graham added with a grimace.

"I take it she won't be at the party with her new husband tonight," Lauren said dryly.

"Into each life some rain must fall."

Lauren couldn't help laughing at his droll intonation. Since Roxanne worked in marketing, Graham was even more a victim of her *confidences* than Lauren was. His responses were invariably short, pithy sayings. He let the rest float over his head.

They were probably being unkind, Lauren thought, as they settled into the car. Spraining an ankle was no joke. It should evoke sympathy. The problem was that Roxanne was such a sympathy gobbler, one's natural store of it ran out. This past year Lauren had taken to actively evading Roxanne and her self-indulgent wallowing in real or imagined woes.

She ruefully reflected that when she had first arrived at Global Publications, she had been sucked right into being a listener. Like a sponge, she had absorbed a steady stream of complaints about the demands and unreasonable expectations of Roxanne's first husband. It had hit on wounds from her own miserable marriage, drawing what might have been, in hindsight, unwarranted sympathy, as well as the best advice she could give.

She hadn't known then that advice was not really what was wanted. Roxanne soaked up advice from everyone who would give it. She went looking for advice constantly because it gave her the excuse to talk about herself. Roxanne Kinsey was the most self-absorbed person Lauren had ever met.

All the same, Roxanne was probably well rid of her first husband. He had sounded as though he was tarred with the same brush as Lauren's big mistake. Men who wanted to own women were innately insecure. No trust. Rabid jealousy. Demanding accountability of every moment away from them. Forcing their will on every little thing.

Nightmare alley, Lauren thought, and was glad to be out of it. Although she did miss living in Melbourne. All her family were there. Unfortunately, so was Wayne, and she didn't trust him to stay out of her life. Despite their divorce, he wouldn't let go. Coming to Sydney had effected a solid break from him, and that had been necessary for her peace of mind, but she did find it lonely up here.

At least she would have a chance to visit her mother during her stay in Melbourne with Evan Daniel. A smile broke through her brooding as she thought of the upcoming promotional tour. Some authors were highly touchy and temperamental, but Evan Daniel was a real sweetie, cheerful, obliging, appreciative of everything she had arranged for

him, a lovely, warm, huggable bear of a man. She
wished she could find someone like him for herself.

Her mobile telephone beeped, and she quickly
drew it out of of her handbag.

Graham threw her a twinkling look. "That thing
will be growing out of your ear if you don't watch
out, Lauren."

"It would be handier if it did," she returned
lightly.

She knew Graham's remark was not a criticism,
yet coming on top of her thoughts about Wayne,
it scraped a highly sensitive area. The night she had
walked away from her marriage, Wayne had ripped
her mobile telephone from her ear and hurled it
against the wall in a jealous rage. The memory
lingered darkly as she answered the call.

It was from the producer of a television daytime
chat show. She had tried to reach him earlier this
afternoon, but he had been too busy to take the
call. He was returning it now. This frequently happened with the media people she had to deal with.
It was not until they had wrapped up the business
of the day that they gave their attention to anything
relating to tomorrow or next week or a fortnight
from now. Calls were made after normal working
hours had ended.

That was one of the reasons Lauren had a mobile
telephone. It was necessary to gain a successful
result from her initiatives. She worked to other
people's convenience, not her own. If she wasn't
available to take calls, to instantly follow up on opportunities offered, they could all too easily be lost.

A promotional campaign had to be effected within a certain limited time. Media interest was often a chain reaction. It was also fickle. If she didn't strike while the iron was hot, she was not doing her job properly. It was as simple as that.

It wasn't as though Wayne hadn't known she loved her job before they were married. It had come as a shock when he had expected her to give it up for him within weeks of their honeymoon. She might even have done so if that had been the only problem emerging between them, but his attitude towards her work permeated everything else, too. It was like having married Dr. Jekyll, then finding herself living with Mr. Hyde.

By the time she had talked through arrangements with the television producer, Graham had driven past King's Cross and was well on the way to Rose Bay. She tucked the mobile phone in her handbag and decided to postpone putting her hair up until they arrived at the restaurant. It would be easier to do it in the ladies' powder room, and they would certainly be arriving ahead of the guests.

"When do you take off with Evan Daniel?" Graham asked.

"Next week. Wednesday."

"You've drummed up a lot of interest in him."

"Good subject."

"He's a nice guy."

"Very likeable," Lauren agreed warmly. "I think he'll come over well. I hope you've got good supplies of his books in the shops, Graham."

"Best-seller status."

"Great!"

He shot her a curious look. "Is Evan Daniel your kind of guy, Lauren?"

"Why do you ask?" she returned teasingly, aware there was considerable speculation about her love life amongst Global's staff.

Graham shrugged. "I know you date occasionally but you don't stick with anyone for long."

"It's difficult to maintain a relationship in my kind of job."

"I notice you shy off really good-looking guys."

"Do I?"

"Yes. And that's odd for a good-looking girl like you."

"Maybe I want more than what's on the surface."

"That's why I asked about Evan."

"He's married, Graham."

"That doesn't seem to stop anyone these days," he observed dryly.

"His wife is pregnant. Do you think I'd respect a man who played around when his wife is expecting his baby?"

"Ah, respect! Yes, there has to be respect." He nodded sagely, then threw her a smile of approval. "I've got to hand it to you, Lauren. You've got your head on straight."

She hoped so. She'd certainly lost her head completely over Wayne. He was so handsome he'd melt most women in their shoes. And he had a body to drool over. Pure pin-up material. Her chemistry had led her badly astray, and that was something to be wary of. Graham was very perceptive. She did shy off good-looking guys.

Maybe, Lauren reflected, that wasn't being fair. One shouldn't make generalisations from one bad experience. She resolved to give the next really attractive man who showed an interest in her at least half a chance to show he had some decent substance, too.

They drove past the marina at Rose Bay and through the gateway to the park where the Salamander Restaurant held a prime position on the shoreline. Global was holding its launching party in real style. Lauren felt a bright lilt of anticipation. Perhaps tonight she would meet someone interesting, a stranger across a crowded room.

She grinned.

Did hope never die?

CHAPTER THREE

LAUREN saw him arrive—the stranger.

She didn't know why her gaze was drawn to the restaurant foyer at that particular moment. She was out on the deck overlooking the bay, chatting with a small circle of associates. People were milling around in the dining room, which had been cleared of its normal furniture for freedom of movement. For some reason the groups of guests had shifted, leaving an unobscured channel of vision. And there he was.

It gave Lauren a weird feeling, as though she had conjured him up herself, somehow waving a mental magic wand, making the people part, and there in the spotlight—one tall, dark, handsome stranger. But the illusion was incomplete. His eyes didn't meet hers. He didn't even glance her way. His attention was directed to his companions. He was smiling, a warm, kindly, reassuring kind of smile.

"Lauren, what did you think of...?"

It took an act of will to draw her gaze to her companions and focus her mind on what was being said. She gave her opinion on the question directed at her and tossed the conversational ball into the general ring, disinterested in pursuing a discussion.

People had moved when she looked again. She surreptitiously changed her position, scanning the

crowd in an idle manner, half wondering at herself
that she felt so drawn to find him, place him.
Hadn't she told herself a thousand times it was the
person inside who really counted, not superficial
attraction?

It was the smile, she decided. She'd liked his
smile. A smile could say a lot about the inner
person. She was curious about him. That was perfectly natural.

She spotted him in a group she quickly ident-
ified. Evan Daniel was talking to his editor, Beth
Hayward. The pretty blonde between Evan and the
stranger was probably Evan's wife, Tasha. She had
a proprietal air as she watched him speak. *My
husband,* it said, with pride and pleasure.

The stranger bent and whispered something in
the blonde's ear. She nodded and threw him a
grateful look. He moved away. Lauren followed his
progress across the room to a set of glass doors that
opened to the other end of the deck from where
she stood. He didn't look around him as most
people did, seeking familiar faces, ready to greet
or respond. From the moment he set off alone, his
face wore a closed, forbidding look.

Lauren was intrigued. It was a total shutdown of
charm. He exuded an air of single-minded purpose.
Not a party animal, she concluded, more a man
with a mission. She wondered why he was here this
evening and what he intended to achieve.

His classy, dark grey suit had the stamp of a con-
servative professional, as did his shirt and neatly
styled black hair. In contrast to that image, a blue

shirt and a brightly patterned silk tie made a vivid splash of individualism that denied any easy pigeonholing of this man.

His face was pleasingly proportioned, cleanly chiseled, unmistakably male, although a full-lipped mouth softened and sensualised it. Another interesting and endearing feature was surprisingly small and neat ears. His eyebrows were straight, with a slightly downward slant. It was impossible to discern eye colour at this distance, but Lauren decided it would probably be brown. Dark chocolate. She loved dark chocolate.

He stepped onto the deck. He didn't glance in her direction or pause to admire the spectacular view of the harbourside around the bay. He headed straight to where tables and chairs were stacked in the far corner. With brisk economy of movement he separated a small table and two chairs, then took them inside, choosing to set them against the glass wall in a protected alcove beside a serving bench.

It was interesting to watch the animation of his face as he returned to Evan and Tasha Daniel, breaking into their chat with Beth Hayward to usher them all over to the place he had prepared for them. As they moved, Lauren saw how heavily pregnant Evan's wife was and realised it was her comfort that was the stranger's prime consideration.

A thoughtful, caring man. Also a man of action. As soon as Tasha Daniel was settled on a chair, he signalled one of the waiters over to offer his tray of drinks. He selected champagne for Tasha but took orange juice for himself. A non-drinker,

Lauren speculated, or a man bent on keeping all his wits about him? It would be interesting to know his connection to Evan and Tasha Daniel.

Lauren waited until Beth Hayward took her leave of them, then went straight into action, intent on having her curiosity satisfied. With the ready excuse of having to see an author, she moved inside and collected two of the gift presentation packs from the display table. Armed with these to sweeten the introduction to Evan's wife and their friend, she headed across the room to them.

Evan saw her coming. His genial face broke into a welcoming smile. He spoke to his wife, clearly identifying Lauren for her, and Tasha Daniel's gaze zeroed in on the woman who would be taking her husband on a promotional tour. Shock was the first reaction. Lauren could almost see, *Her?* flashing into Tasha's mind, surrounded by neon-red lights zigzagging danger signals.

She'd met the reaction before and hoped to defuse it quickly. Few women liked the idea of having Lauren look after their men. She was too vividly female, almost spectacularly so with the contrast of pearly pale skin, copper-red hair and cornflower-blue eyes. But she was not a predatory rival for their affections. Usually she managed to project that, given a few minutes in their company.

After leaving Wayne, she had gone through a period of downplaying her physical attributes, covering up her figure, wearing no make-up, even having her red curls cropped to within an inch of her scalp and dying her hair brown, hating the idea of any man seeing her only as an ornamental possession.

Eventually she had realised she was damaging herself, feeding fears and repressing her natural exuberance for life and all its joys. It was much better to simply maintain a balanced sense of self-worth and let the rest of the world sort itself out.

Lauren felt the stranger watch her approach, too. Maybe it was only the effect of her heightened awareness of him, but she was conscious of all her sensory levels rising, sharpening, as though she was moving into a highly dangerous zone. Suddenly she felt wary of him, reluctant to pursue the interest he had sparked in her.

A spurious, fantasy interest, she told herself, bound to bring disappointment. Now that she was so close, it was silly not to look and assess the man more directly, yet some deeply protective instinct tugged on her mind, wanting to shun the influence he had already unwittingly exerted on her. She switched on a bright smile for Evan Daniel and his wife, but didn't include the stranger in its warm sweep. He was, after all, a stranger.

"Hi, there!" she greeted them with casual friendliness. "I collected these souvenirs for you before they're all taken."

"I didn't realise they were being given away," Evan remarked in surprise. "Thanks, Lauren. Good of you to think of it." He turned quickly to his wife, who began to struggle up from her chair. "This is Tasha. Lauren Magee, Tasha."

"Please don't move," Lauren protested. "It's good you've found a place to sit. It's a long night on one's feet."

"Yes," Tasha agreed, subsiding again. "I'm pleased to meet you, Lauren," she added somewhat stiffly.

"Likewise. I've heard so much about you from Evan. And the coming baby. I'm very happy for you both."

Tasha flushed. "Thank you."

"And please remember, if you're worried about anything while Evan is away on tour, just ring me on my mobile telephone number, and I'll cancel interviews at a moment's notice. You come first, Tasha."

The wariness left her eyes. "Oh, I'm sure everything will be all right."

"That's great! Your husband has written a topline book, so we hope to let every reader in Australia hear about it."

"I'm amazed at the number of interviews you've lined up for him."

Lauren laughed, placing the catalogue and T-shirt packages on the table for Tasha to take as she shared her amusement in a woman-to-woman confidence. "He'll be complaining to you about being run off his feet and how exhausted he is, but it will be worth the effort if the sales zoom. That's the whole point of the exercise."

"How soon will you know if it's worked?" she asked curiously.

Having successfully refocused Tasha's mind, taking it off her and moving it squarely onto the job in hand, Lauren relaxed. "Give it a month." She moved her gaze to Evan. "If you contact Graham Parker, of marketing, he should have figures for you by then."

"Oh, good! Uh, Lauren..." Relief and pleasure beamed from Evan's face. With the eagerness of an overgrown puppy wanting everyone lapped with goodwill, he pressed on. "Someone I want you to meet."

She braced herself. Against what, she wasn't sure. Even as she'd been addressing Tasha, working at winning her over, she had been acutely conscious of the man standing to the right of her, waiting, listening, watching.

Evan gestured for her to turn and meet the stranger head on. "My friend and literary agent, Michael Timberlane."

Lauren's mind buzzed with that information as she slowly swung towards him. Michael Timberlane was, by renown, the most trusted literary agent in the business, his judgment of books being proved commercially sound so many times it overrode doubt. She knew he handled Evan's work and that of many other successful authors, but their paths had never crossed.

His work was done before she was called in to help the books sell. She hadn't been curious about him, since his field of expertise didn't touch on hers. But she was curious now. The combination of a

highly perceptive mind in a highly attractive body
was an irresistible draw.

Still an instinctive caution held her back from
showing eagerness. She fixed a polite smile on her
face, one she would turn on for an introduction to
anyone. Her gaze, she was sure, reflected only a
friendly interest as she lifted it to acknowledge him.

Choong! Two laser beams piercing her eyes and
attacking her soul with lightning-bolt force!

Lauren felt like a stunned butterfly, pinned to a
board for minute examination under a powerful
microscope and utterly helpless to do anything
about it. She had not braced herself enough. She
vaguely sensed a declaration of war—*you cannot
hide from me*—and the assault from his eyes—
silver-grey eyes, like luminous stainless steel slicing
through all her defensive levels—left her mind
quivering and her body a mass of jangling nerve
ends.

She must have offered her hand because she felt
it being taken, hard warmth enclosing hers, male
touching female, igniting an electric sense of sexuality, linking, testing, while his eyes still staked their
claim on her, riveting in their concentrated quest
for knowledge. And she couldn't tear her own away.

Lauren had never experienced anything like it in
her whole life. Some tiny logical strain in her brain
recited that this cataclysmic moment would pass.
It had to. Time did move on. Soon she would make
sense of this.

Soon . . .

CHAPTER FOUR

MICHAEL fought grimly against being completely thrown by the woman who stood before him. His first sight of her had been like a punch in the gut. Lauren Magee was everything Evan had said she was, and more—gorgeous, sexy, vibrant, vital, and that was before she had even opened her mouth and displayed the adept mind that could assess a situation, seize it and act positively to gain the result she wanted.

Tasha was now putty in her hands. Evan's fears were demolished. It was perfectly plain he was tickled pink by the attention Lauren Magee was giving to both of them. And it was such clever attention, striking the right note of caring and liking for Tasha and a delightfully open camaraderie with Evan.

Michael had clutched at cynicism to reduce her effect on him. Lauren Magee was exerting control over her impact, exercising manipulative skills, showing she was a superior being who could handle anything and anyone. Not him, he had fiercely vowed as she had turned to encompass him in her powerful radiance. He knew her for what she was!

With every atom of his brain and will he had penetrated the deceptive mask of polite interest, denying the distraction of her stunning blue eyes,

seeking for the truth, scouring her soul for it. There
had to be some trace of antagonism towards him,
some sense of malicious triumph. She knew who
he was now. She had to know what part she had
played in ending his marriage.

Nothing! Nothing except a mesmerised wonder
that tugged at his heart, making him feel like a
marauding savage for not treating her tenderly. That
had to be wrong. She was tricking him somehow.

He took hold of her hand, grasping it firmly, expecting at least a twinge of recoil. If she was true
to her inner beliefs and judgments she had to react
negatively to his touch. Yet her hand lay submis-
sively in his, soft, delicately boned, seductively
feminine, stirring sensations he didn't want to
acknowledge.

Still that clear luminosity in her eyes. Nothing to
hide. But there had to be. Unless . . .

She didn't know he was Roxanne's ex-husband.

It seemed incredible to Michael that Lauren
Magee was ignorant of the connection, yet it was
the only answer that made sense of her total lack
of any discernible rejection of him. Had Roxanne
been so disaffected that she hadn't bothered to
identify him as the husband she sought advice
about?

Keeping her precious maiden name of Kinscy
might have muddled the tracks, or Roxanne could
have assumed it was common knowledge she was
married to Michael Timberlane. She had been
proud to own him for the first year or two, though
by the time Lauren Magee arrived in Sydney from

Melbourne, the shine had worn off that pride under
the burden of trying to make their relationship gel
in a workable fashion.

Easier for Roxanne to slide out of putting the
effort in, Michael reflected cynically, and Lauren
Magee had given her all the excuses to justify doing
so. Yet she looked at him so innocently, so openly
and honestly, waiting for him to write on the blank
sheet that the meeting of strangers always offered,
to give her a cue for what might develop between
them from this moment, a moment cut free of any
past and offering all the choices of possible futures.

He was tempted.

In any rational, objective sense, Lauren Magee
was an anathema to him.

Yet he wanted her.

He wanted to empty her mind of all its clever
reasoning and drive her insane with desire for him.
He wanted to unpin the fiery mass of curls she had
swirled into a topknot and see them spilling over a
pillow in riotous abandonment. He wanted to tear
off her sweater and fill his hands with the lush
softness of those delectably rounded breasts that
were thrusting so provocatively against the stretchy
knit fabric.

And that sexy belt accentuating the feminine
smallness of her waist and the sensual curve of her
hips... He imagined stretching her white-skinned
arms above her head, winding the wide black elastic
around her wrists with the gold bow on top, holding
her hands together so she couldn't weave her female
magic on him while he took his fill of her.

Lauren Magee, submitting to the man she had reviled, giving herself to him, her long, elegant legs wrapped around him in supplication, in need, wanting him . . . Oh, yes, that would be sweet vengeance. And ravishing her luscious mouth, purging it of all the unjust words she'd said against him, replacing them with the intensely satisfying sounds of cries and gasps of pleasure.

His loins tightened. His heart thudded with the violent force of the warring feelings she stirred. His body zinged with shots of adrenaline as his mind played through one scenario after another, all of them erotic, all of them feeding the highly aroused savage inside him.

It took all of Michael's formidable willpower to clamp down on that rampant beast. Basic common sense insisted he play the civilised man. Fantasies were fantasies. Realities wiped out any chance of them happening anyway.

He might be a blank page to Lauren Magee right now, but the moment Roxanne turned up, he'd be history in her book. Roxanne would make certain of it. He only had a very limited time to play the game he had set out to play, getting in a few pointed shots that might just puncture Lauren Magee's confidence in dabbling with other people's lives.

It should be amusing to draw her out, to watch her natural response to him before Roxanne's axe fell. And afterwards she would remember. Oh, yes, that keen, clever mind of Lauren Magee's would remember everything said between them, spoken and unspoken.

Michael told himself he would be satisfied with that. The trick was to keep his mind focused on the desired result, the only result that was really open to him.

CHAPTER FIVE

"I'M IMPRESSED."

Michael Timberlane's voice seemed to harmonise with the feelings he stirred, sliding to Lauren on a low, penetrating, intimate level.

"What by?" The words tripped from her tongue, breathless, husky, unconsidered, revealing how deeply she was caught in the thrall of possibilities pulsing between them.

"Your professionalism," he answered.

Did he know intuitively what was important to her? Excitement tingled through a welling of intense pleasure. Lauren wished she knew more of him. Was he married?

"Thank you," she returned warmly. "I do my best. As you do, by reputation."

"There are some who would say my best falls short of their expectations. Haven't you heard that, Ms. Magee?"

His hand slid away from hers. The withdrawal highlighted the unexpected formality of his address to her. Lauren felt confused. Why was he suddenly being off-putting?

"I'm sorry if you've been a target of ill will, Mr. Timberlane," she said with a touch of sympathy. "People's expectations are sometimes unrealistic."

"And unreasonable," he shot back.

37

She hesitated, uncertain of where he was coming from or leading to. Wayne and his unreasonable expectations flitted through her mind. Maybe Michael Timberlane was still smarting from some personal or professional contretemps. With someone at Global? Was that what had made him look so forbidding earlier?

Lauren fell back on one of Graham Parker's pithy sayings, offering it with an ironic little smile. "Well, Mr. Timberlane, I guess into each life some rain must fall."

"You being the rainmaker?"

She laughed and shook her head. "I like to think I spread sunshine."

"The giver of light." He nodded, his silvery eyes gleaming satisfaction. "Yes, that would be how you think of yourself."

"And how do you think of yourself, Mr. Timberlane?"

He smiled, but it was a secretive, private smile, not an open, sharing one. "Oh, I'm the sword of justice, Ms. Magee."

Definitely on some personal high horse, Lauren thought, wanting to pull him down from it. "Then I hope your balancing scales are in good order. Justice is so often blind," she said, tilting at him.

"How true!" he agreed. "It's unfortunate that so many people's eyes aren't open to both sides of a situation before making judgments."

"Are yours?"

"I always look at the big picture, Ms. Magee."

"Never missing a piece of the jigsaw, Mr. Timberlane?" she queried, niggled by his assumption of having all-seeing eyes. Nobody saw everything.

"Oh, for heaven's sake!" Evan broke in jocularly. "What's all this Mr. and Ms.? We're at a party, not a stuffy reception."

"One must be careful not to assume too much these days, Evan," Michael Timberlane answered his friend good-humouredly. "How do I know I'm not meeting a raging feminist who'll take offence at inappropriate familiarity?"

Evan laughed. "I'd think it's obvious Lauren isn't a raging feminist."

"Appearances can be deceptive." Michael raised his eyebrows quizzically at Lauren. "Would you be so kind as to shed some light on the matter?"

Why did she have the sense he was playing out some secret agenda, toying with her, waiting to pounce if she didn't keep on her toes?

"You have my permission to call me Lauren," she said with a disarming smile, neatly sidestepping any argument about feminism.

"Then I shall not stand upon dignity," he replied with mock gravity. "Please feel free to call me Michael."

Lauren laughed at him. There was a certain spice to the game, a challenge. She couldn't recall any man ever having put her quite so much on her mettle before, certainly not at first meeting.

"I've never liked Ms.," Tasha remarked artlessly. "It sounds like a mosquito."

"I think that's spoken from the complacency of being a Mrs., Tasha," Michael reproved lightly. "Lauren may feel differently."

Another test, another nudge.

Tasha flushed, her brown eyes shining an apologetic appeal. "I'm sorry. I didn't think. I guess it has its place."

There was a fragile vulnerability, a simple innocence about Tasha Daniel that automatically touched Lauen's protective instinct. She was not street-wise, and with Evan as her husband had probably never had the need to become so. In a way, Lauren envied that, never having to confront the darker games men and women played.

"It saves making a mistake with Miss or Mrs.," she gently explained. "Like Mr., it doesn't carry the label of being single or married."

"Will you keep Ms. when you do marry?" Tasha asked curiously.

"That's assuming she wants to marry," Michael pointed out. "Many career women choose not to take on a commitment that could interfere with their life goals."

"Oh, dear!" Tasha pulled a rueful grimace. "I'm really putting my foot in it, aren't I?"

Lauren smiled to set her at ease again. "Being politically correct can be carried too far. I don't mind your questions, Tasha. I've been married, and I was very happy to be a Mrs. then."

Michael's face jerked towards her. Surprise. Reappraisal. Lauren had a sense of factors being shifted, energy zapping through him as his inner vision was rearranged.

"Now I'm divorced," she went on matter-of-factly, "the title of Miss is fine by me."

Tasha looked pained. "Another broken marriage. Michael's been through it, too. So sad..."

One revelation had bought another.

Michael Timberlane was divorced—single—free! The equation zipped through Lauren's brain, and she didn't feel sad at all. She felt as though wonderful fireworks were exploding in fabulous cascades of brilliant colour, lighting up a world that had been empty of dreams.

She was twenty-nine, looking down the barrel of thirty. Unattached, intriguing and attractive men like Michael Timberlane weren't exactly thick on the ground. Attractive was far too weak a word, she swiftly corrected. He was dynamite. He had both her mind and body shaken to acute awareness of all sorts of exciting possibilities.

Hope was definitely not dead!

"No reason to be sad, Tasha," Michael said. "It's a matter of statistics in today's society. Two out of three marriages end in divorce. You and Evan are the lucky ones. You should let us in on the secrets of your success."

Tasha smiled and reached out her hand to her husband. "It's wanting the same things," she said with moving simplicity. "Isn't it, Evan?"

"Yes," he agreed, beaming his love at her as he took her hand and fondled it indulgently.

Lauren fought down an emotional lump in her throat. They were lucky to have found what they wanted in each other. She wondered what had gone wrong with Michael Timberlane's marriage. Who had left whom, and why?

"I didn't know you'd been married, Lauren," Evan commented with a look of puzzlement at her.

She shrugged, inwardly recoiling from that bad time. "Does anyone like talking about their mistakes?"

Evan shook his head. "I can't imagine why any man wouldn't fight tooth and nail to keep you with him."

"I'll take that as a compliment," she said, smiling to hide the bitter irony behind it. Wayne had certainly fought to keep her with him. Abusively. On a sudden wave of fear, she turned to Michael Timberlane and bluntly asked, "Did you fight to keep your wife?"

For one fleeting moment she saw a turbulent core of savagery flash through the windows of his soul. It sent a shiver down her spine. Then the silver screen of his extraordinarily compelling eyes clicked into place again, glistening with outward interest in her, reflecting nothing of what was within.

"It's difficult to fight a saboteur," he said with a sardonic twist. "The damage is done behind one's back."

He'd hate that, she thought.

"Besides, when the illusion of love and commitment has proven false, why fight to keep it?"

he went on. "I'm a great believer in facing realities and moving on."

"Yes," she agreed, elated that he shared her attitude and convictions.

But it was one thing to leave the experience behind, another to forget. She wondered what damage he carried, what his wife had been like, why she had taken a lover? The reference to a saboteur pointed to another man in her life, and infidelity certainly destroyed the illusion of love and commitment.

"Do let's get off this painful subject," Tasha pleaded. "I wish I hadn't brought it up. This is a happy night."

"Indeed it is!" Lauren quickly supported her, switching on a bright smile. She didn't want this electric sense of anticipation tarnished by memories of relationships that had failed to bring the happiness they had initially promised. Determined not to brood on her past or Michael's, she turned teasingly to Evan. "I'm looking forward to your speech. It's your first public tryout, and I don't expect you to disappoint."

Evan pulled a doleful look. "Pressure, pressure. My editor said the same thing. My wife wants me to shine. Michael thinks I don't need his applause..."

"I promise to clap if no one else does," Michael interposed.

"It's a wonderful speech," Tasha declared. "I know, because he's been rehearsing to me."

"Such loyalty is the voice of love, my darling,"
Evan said, almost purring. "And I appreciate it. I
truly do."

They bantered on in light party style. Waitresses
circulated with fancy finger food, Melba toast with
smoked salmon, fish cocktails, spicy chicken legs,
mini croissants with savoury fillings. Both Evan and
Tasha helped themselves liberally, enjoying the
novelty. Lauren wondered if Michael's stomach was
in the same state as hers. Both of them declined
everything offered.

"Dieting?" Michael asked at one point.

"No." She looked directly into his eyes. "Are
you?"

"No."

There was a magnetic flash of unspoken but un-
mistakable recognition and understanding. Their
hunger was for other things.

But would it be answered?

Lauren stayed at his side, wanting to know more
of Michael Timberlane.

He was charm itself to Tasha and obviously a
supportive friend to Evan, yet for the most part,
he remained a tantalising enigma to her. The sexual
attraction was strong and mutual. Nothing else
could explain the vibrant energy field being generated between them. But she'd felt an awareness akin
to this with Wayne and knew it could be treacherous. Perhaps Michael had similar thoughts, reflecting on his experience with his ex-wife.

Was the control he was exerting simply caution
on his part, or did it conceal something darker?

Was she flirting with danger? Was she willing to take a risk on pursuing this fascination with a stranger? Handsome men were usually spoilt men, she reminded herself, their egos too well fed from always getting their own way.

But Michael had shown consideration to Tasha.

Lauren found herself pushing caution aside and justifying the case for ignoring it altogether. For so long now she had trodden a safe path, and where had it led her? She was lonely. It was not a happy state, being lonely.

She wanted this excitement, this sense of being on the brink of something special. It was exhilarating. She felt so alive. She wanted to turn to Michael Timberlane and say, *Don't hide from me,* but she wasn't quite bold enough to do it. Besides, if he was the man for her, he would decide to involve himself further without any pushing.

She willed him to want to.

"Evan..." Beth Hayward, Evan's editor, broke into their foursome. "They're getting ready for the speeches." She smiled at the glass in his hand. "Had enough drinks to fortify you?"

She was six years older than Lauren, a striking brunette, stylish and very much a woman of the world. She wore a long grey skirt and a cowl top in black and white and grey. It was a smart, fashionable, sophisticated outfit. Lauren glanced at Michael, sensing a sudden coiling of tension in him.

His face had hardened, wearing the same closed expression she had noted earlier when he had left

Beth with the Daniels to collect the table and chairs. Was there some conflict between them? They would have done business together many times, since Beth was a commissioning editor for Global.

"I feel warm and convivial but definitely not fuzzy," Evan declared. "Where am I wanted?"

Beth nodded towards the bar. "Up that end of the room." She smiled at Michael. "Perhaps you could bring a chair for Tasha, because they'll probably go on for a while."

"We'll look after her comfort," Lauren assured Evan, coupling herself with Michael.

Beth darted a sharply speculative look between Lauren and Michael, then frowned as though niggled by some problem. Her gaze fell on the gift packages, still lying on the table. "I see you've collected your souvenirs. Better not leave them behind," she advised. "They're all gone from the display table."

"I'll take them with me," Tasha said, quickly gathering them up.

Beth looked directly at Lauren with a curious expression that seemed to convey some loaded meaning. "A pity Roxanne sprained her ankle this afternoon and couldn't come to the party. Do you know—"

Crash! Broken glass and spilled wine scattered and splashed across the floor right next to Michael. A drinks tray had toppled from a waiter's hand, and the people closest to the disaster area scuttled back with cries of shock and dismay at being spattered.

Michael wheeled and gestured an apologetic appeal at the hapless waiter. "I'm so sorry! Did I bump you?"

"Not to worry, sir. These things happen with a crowd."

"Let me help." He crouched to pick up the tray.

"No, please leave it, sir," the waiter protested emphatically. "Staff will be here in a moment to do the necessary."

"Damn! Red wine on my skirt!" Beth muttered in vexation. "Excuse me, I'm off to the powder room. Evan, don't dally. It's time to move." She didn't wait for him, frustration and impatience with the mishap getting the better of courtesy.

Michael straightened and pulled a rueful grimace. "Not my best party trick."

"Well, it can't be helped now," Tasha said sympathetically. "Do go on, Evan. Michael and Lauren will see to me."

"Front row seat," Michael promised. He clapped his friend on the shoulder. "Off you toddle, and mind you do us proud." He grinned, his face lighting up with undiluted good humour. "You can hold up the bar until you're wanted for your party piece."

Lauren couldn't help staring at the startling transformation a wicked grin made to Michael Timberlane's face. She had thought him handsome before, certainly enough to spark her interest at first sight of him. But the difference now was heart-stopping. A grin like that would cause any woman considerable internal havoc. Lauren was no exception.

She vaguely heard Evan and Tasha exchange a few words, then Evan started weaving his way through the crowd and Michael turned to her, the grin still lurking, his silver eyes gleaming with some wild and reckless satisfaction that instantly encompassed her.

Her pulse kicked into a faster beat. Her mind throbbed with the knowledge he was going to ride the current that flowed between them. No more stand off. No pulling back. He had decided.

She felt the glow of a wild and reckless satisfaction grow inside herself. She had willed this from him. *So let it be,* she thought, *wherever it might lead.*

She repressed the thought that it could be dangerous.

She didn't wonder, Why now? What had changed from a few moments ago?

She made no connection whatsoever between Michael Timberlane's decision and the accidental tipping over of a tray.

She forgot about Beth Hayward and whatever she was going to tell her about Roxanne.

She was brilliantly, vibrantly, idiotically happy!

CHAPTER SIX

MICHAEL could barely tear his eyes away from her to make the coffee. Lauren Magee in his apartment, not wanting the night to end any more than he did. Not the Lauren of *Lauren says*. It was utterly absurd to even vaguely relate this woman to Roxanne's ally in castrating men.

False impressions, lies... He shook his head, dismissing them all. The reality was this magical enchantress who offered him everything he'd ever dreamed of in a woman. Her openness delighted him. Her intelligence, her uninhibited sexuality, her honest expression and acceptance of her feelings made her incredibly special.

Maybe he should tell her about Roxanne, get it out of the way. But Lauren hadn't brought up her ex-husband. Those marriages were mistakes. Neither of them had known what it could be like with the right person. As Lauren had said to Evan, nobody likes talking about their mistakes. Why waste time that could be better spent exploring what was happening between them?

"You are so lucky to have such a fantastic view! she said with a long, appreciative sigh.

Yes, he thought, looking at her drinking in the harbour vista through the floor-to-ceiling windows in his sunken living room. The opera house, the bridge, the watercraft in and out of Circular Quay provided a feast of glittering spectacles, but she outshone them. Her shoes were off, her glorious hair unpinned, the seductive curves of her femininity silhouetted in soft lamplight, and he whimsically wondered if she'd ever been painted. He mentally ran through the artists he knew. Who could do her justice?

She turned to look at him behind the kitchen counter on the mezzanine level. ''Are you terribly rich, Michael?'' she asked.

No-one had ever asked that question quite so frankly. He grinned at her, amused by her total lack of artfulness. ''Should I admit it or conceal it?''

''Are you wondering what effect your reply will have on me?''

''I suspect, none.''

She laughed. ''I'm not here for your money. I said yes to your invitation before I even knew you drove a BMW. But such an expensive car and this apartment, both of which you seem to take for granted...''

''Does that offend you?''

''No.'' She shrugged. ''I just want to know about you.''

He pressed the plunger on the coffee grains as he considered how best to answer.

''Does it bother you, Michael?'' she asked quietly.

''I guess rich is the wrong word. I have never felt rich...until tonight.'' He met her gaze and spoke the truth as he knew it. ''To be rich is to have things of great value, Lauren. I've never valued wealth because I've had it all my life and it can't give you what you really want."

"Are we talking great wealth here?"

"Mmm..." He poured out the coffee, picked up the tray he'd set and carried it down to the living room. "Goes back to the last century. The Timberlanes were highly successful merchants. Owned ships and docking yards and auction houses. Lots of investments in city property and businesses."

Lauren frowned. "But you're not a high-profile family. I've never heard or read about you in that sense."

"A very quiet establishment family," he agreed. "Besides, I'm the only one left living in Australia. I have a brother who prefers Monaco and an aunt who has long been settled in Italy."

She looked appalled. "What happened to the rest of your family?"

"Wealth does not prevent death." He set the tray on a glass table. "Cream? Sugar?"

She helped herself. They settled on one of the leather chesterfields and she regarded him pensively. "Why a literary agent?"

"I like encouraging authors and getting their books published. They give a lot of pleasure to others."

He would never have survived his boyhood without books and the escape they provided, not with any sanity, but he didn't want to rake over those old nightmares. He didn't want her sympathy. He wanted her warmth, the total inner essence of Lauren Magee.

"Do you come from a large family?" he asked.

"Yes." She laughed. "Five brothers and three sisters, plus innumerable aunts and uncles and cousins. You could say the Magees went forth and multiplied at a profligate rate. They all have big families."

"Then you can count yourself as very rich, indeed."

"Yes. Though I . . ." She checked herself. "Well, I'll get to see them soon. I'm glad you're not an idle playboy. I like my work, too."

"Tell me how you got into it," he invited, genuinely interested in knowing.

"Communication, public relations . . ."

She talked about the various jobs she'd held, moving up to publicist for a publisher. A natural progression, Michael thought, and pondered the one telling comment that her ex-husband had disliked her work. The man could not have really loved her. Anyone with eyes could see that Lauren lived and breathed the publicity mill. Using it as brilliantly as she obviously did was an expression of herself, her unique talents and abilities.

She was such a joy to watch, so vital, her eyes the blue of summer skies bathing him with sparkling sunshine, heating him with a simmering brew of desires he could barely contain. The right woman. Coming from a big family, she would be sure to want children herself. Beautiful breasts. Voluptuous hips. Long, elegant, sexy legs. She could even match him dancing. Everything right.

The urge to reach out and pull her into full body contact with him made his hands itch. She had to feel the need, too. The coffee was cold in their cups, forgotten, untouched by either of them. If she wanted to leave, she would have said so by now. Was it assuming too much to want everything on the first night?

Let there be truth between us, he thought with passionate intensity as he stood and took her hands, drawing her to her feet and into a loose embrace that didn't demand or presume. Her eyes were wide, waiting for him to speak his mind, her body softly pliant, no resistance. The desire raging through him could not be denied.

"I want you, Lauren," he said, his voice raw with urgency.

"Yes," she answered with a soft expulsion of breath.

"Are you protected?"

"No."

"I'll take care of it."

"I'd appreciate that."

So direct, so honest in her desire for him. It almost blew Michael's mind, as well as other strained parts of his anatomy. He lifted a hand to touch the softness of her cheek, trailed his fingers into the silken curls of her hair. Her lips parted invitingly. Her eyes swam with hopes and dreams.

"Not here," he said gruffly, barely recognising his own voice. "Come all the way with me, Lauren."

"Yes."

He led her upstairs to his bedroom.

Her mouth was passion.

Her hair was erotic sensuality.

Her breasts were intoxicating.

Her hands were hypnotic pleasure.

Her legs were seductive silk.

And the inner essence of Lauren Magee . . . was ecstasy.

Michael loved her as he'd never loved a woman before, with unbridled passion, uninhibited fervour, wild exultation and the freedom—the amazingly sweet freedom—of fulfilling his every desire and meeting always the most exquisite response. Perfection. Bliss. Pleasure on a scale he had never imagined possible. And she gave it him. Lauren. The woman of his dreams.

It made up for everything else—the neglect of his parents who had never been there for him and his younger brother, Peter, even when they were alive; the oppression of his childhood under the cold domination of his grandmother; the loneliness of boarding school; the sense of not belonging at Oxford and Harvard; the alienation from his brother, who saw no point in working at anything; the bitter disillusionment of his marriage to Roxanne.

He should tell Lauren about Roxanne.

Tomorrow.

Tonight belonged to them. The future belonged to them. He could see it, taste it, feel it. And it was right.

CHAPTER SEVEN

THE morning after... The phrase flitted through Lauren's mind as she rode to work on the bus, and she almost laughed out loud at its connotations of shock and regrets and subsequent blues. None of it applied to how she felt.

It was as though her bloodstream was bubbling with joy. A sparkling zest for life sharpened all her senses. She was in love—madly, deliciously, wonderfully in love—and she didn't regret one moment of the risks she had taken. Not one.

This time yesterday, if someone had told her she would meet a man, fall head over heels in love and go to bed with him, all on the same night, she would have responded to the prediction with outright disbelief. No chance. She wasn't that kind of woman. She had her head on straight. Impulsive sexual adventures were not her style, never had been, never would be. Making love should be something special with someone special.

And it had been. Lauren closed her eyes and hugged the memory of all the marvellous sensations Michael had made her feel. He was a fantastic lover, wildly passionate, incredibly sensual, erotic and tender, powerful and playful. Lauren had never known a night like it. Wayne... But she wasn't going to think about her ex-husband any more. Her life had definitely taken an upward turn with Michael Timberlane.

She wondered if she should have woken him before leaving his apartment this morning. It had been tempting, just to share a last kiss, a last smile, the mutual knowledge of how incredibly magical their coming together had been. But he would have delayed her, and she'd barely had time enough to whiz to the house she shared at Chatswood, change her clothes for work and catch her usual bus to Artarmon. Besides, the note she had left him said it all.

The bus came to a ponderous halt. It was her stop. Lauren leapt from her seat and pushed quickly past the standing passengers to the opened door. She alighted on the sidewalk with a spring in her step and only just suppressed the urge to skip and twirl down the street to her office building.

Michael had danced her off her feet last night. He was the best. The very best. At everything! She was so lucky to have met him, lucky the attraction was mutual, lucky to be alive and sharing the world Michael Timberlane occupied.

A song started playing through her mind. It was "I Feel Pretty" from *West Side Story*. Only last week she'd seen the revival of the original stage production, currently showing at the Capital Theatre. She remembered the exhilaration coursing through Maria following her meeting with Tony, the high spirits that had fired the song with its lovely lilt of exhuberant happiness. It was precisely how Lauren felt.

She was still singing it in her head as she entered Global's foyer and walked jauntily to the elevators. The receptionist, Sue Carroll, spotted her and called out, "Hey! That was some hot dancing last night, Lauren. How did you latch onto Michael Timberlane?"

"He was with Evan Daniel," Lauren answered offhandedly, unwilling to feed Sue's penchant for gossip.

"Of course. Your current project." Sue's smile was a twist of irony. "Well, the macho Michael sure surprised me, loosening up like that. The few times he's come through here, you'd think he was encased in ice. Cold, forbidding and untouchable."

His manner had undoubtedly piqued her. Sue enjoyed a bit of chitchat and loved to know everybody's business. Apart from that, no attractive young woman, even married as Sue was, liked to be frozen out by a handsome man. With her chic pageboy bob and shiny brown eyes, pretty face and petite figure, Sue tended to court male attention and usually got it.

"Maybe the party atmosphere thawed him," Lauren suggested tactfully as the elevator doors opened.

"Or something more basic."

Lauren laughed off the dry comment and hurried into the compartment, waving to Sue while pressing the button for her floor and exulting with private certainty that it was she who had melted the ice. It was interesting, though, that Sue had been subjected to the forbidding look Lauren had observed last night. Obviously Michael didn't open up to many people, but when he did . . . Lauren breathed a sweet sigh of satisfaction. Dynamite!

She walked briskly from the elevator to her office, happy to return greetings from fellow workers but not encouraging any discourse about last night's party. No-one would understand what had happened between herself and Michael, and she didn't want to make light of it. There would inevitably be comments like Sue Carroll's to field. For the moment, however, Lauren preferred to defer them.

Once in her office, she switched on her computer, collected the faxes that had come in and settled at her desk. Her inner happiness bubbled up again at the memory of Michael's appreciation of her work. He knew how important good promotion was in launching a new book on the market. Far from denigrating or resenting or dismissing her job, as Wayne had, Michael had shown he would be right behind her in everything she tried to achieve.

To be able to talk freely about it, to share ideas with someone who was receptive and constructive in bouncing ideas back . . . that was sheer heaven to Lauren. It was wonderful to have books in common. For Michael, too, it was surely more pleasurable to be with a woman who comprehended what his business entailed.

Though there were plenty of women in the publishing industry who would be attuned to it. Like Beth Hayward. Recalling Michael's tension at Beth's approach last night, Lauren wondered if

there had been something between them. Not that
it mattered now.

Having dismissed the speculation, Lauren
skimmed through the faxes, noting replies that had
to be made and appointments that had to be
changed. She was updating her schedules when
Graham Parker dropped by, bringing her a cup of
coffee.

"Nursing a hangover?" he asked, looking
somewhat seedy himself.

She smiled. "No, but thanks for the thought."

He set her mug carefully on the desk then sagged
slowly onto the spare chair, holding his own mug
gingerly. "Oh, to be young and full of boundless
energy," he intoned.

"I take it you overindulged."

"They were serving a very good red."

Lauren knew his wife was to have met him at the
party, so no doubt she had driven him home. "Well,
so long as it was worth it," she said, barely repressing outright amusement at his hangdog
expression.

He gave her a doleful look. "I hope it was for
you, too."

"I'm not suffering," she reminded him.

"You will. Believe me, you will."

His conviction puzzled her. "How so?"

"I know Roxanne. The classic dog-in-the-manger
attitude will click in the moment she hears."

"Hears what?"

He frowned at her as though she was definitely
thick in the head. "Correct me if I'm wrong, dear

girl, but were you not tripping the light fantastic with Michael Timberlane last night? Or should I say, exploring the modern boundaries of dirty dancing?''

Lauren grinned. "He's certainly got rhythm."

"Yes. My wife considered him as good as John Travolta. A high accolade, indeed, considering how many times she's watched what she calls classic Travolta movies."

The sardonic comment did not enlighten her. "So what point are you making, Graham?"

"Oh, far be it from me to question chemistry. If you want to get involved with Michael Timberlane, that's entirely your business. I merely perceive the thunderclouds gathering on the horizon." He sighed. "I guess I'm going to get rained on again."

"Why should you?"

"Because Roxanne won't like it, and she'll pour out her umpteen million reasons, and as her closest associate, I'll cop it more than you will. She might not have any use for her ex-husband, but I very much doubt she'll take kindly to—"

"Her *ex-husband*?" Shock and incredulity billowed through Lauren's mind.

"You didn't know he was He Who Demandeth Too Much?" Graham was startled out of his air of bleak resignation.

"Michael Timberlane is Mikey the Monster?" Lauren squeaked, her voice rising uncontrollably as her mind fought to relate the man she had met last night to the husband who had made Roxanne miserable. The two images simply did not mesh in any shape or form.

"The Dump Merchant," Graham expounded, nodding gravely.

"How could she call him Mikey?" It was a cry of protest against what she didn't want to accept.

"A need to diminish him. The guy is formidable. Roxanne couldn't live up to him. Simple psychology," Graham answered in his best pithy style.

"But..." Lauren floundered, shattered by her ignorance. "Her name is Kinsey."

"Maiden name. It's still Kinsey, even though she's married again," Graham pointed out. "Roxanne clings to it because it has status. Being from Melbourne, you're probably not aware that generations of Kinseys have held high office in the New South Wales government. Kinsey equals power. Timberlane is also old establishment, but most of that family has died off. Not very useful for Roxanne, who got her job here because someone who knew someone..."

Lauren groaned, appalled that probably everyone on Global's staff had been titillated by her social involvement with Roxanne's ex-husband, doubly appalled that she could have been so completely misled by a man who, according to Roxanne, was every bit as soul-crushing as Wayne.

"Sorry." Graham offered a rueful grimace. "I thought you were being brave."

"Stupidly reckless, you mean."

"Not necessarily. Horses for courses. You're made of sterner stuff than Roxanne."

"Not that stern." Her eyes flashed bitter determination. "I'm through with fighting to be me. I don't need another bout of it, thank you very much."

"Oh, I wouldn't take too much notice of Roxanne's self-serving diatribes against him," Graham said dryly. "She didn't really want a man. She wanted a sugar daddy. And that's precisely what she's married now."

Lauren was not consoled. The blissful confidence she'd had in her response to Michael Timberlane was in tatters. Gone were her buoyant spirits. Gone were her high hopes. Was she doomed to be attracted to the wrong kind of man? Perhaps it was Roxanne who had her head on straight, choosing a sugar daddy who was happy to give her everything she wanted in return for simply being herself with him.

Graham pushed himself up from the chair and gestured apologetically. "I didn't mean to drop a bombshell on you, Lauren."

"That's okay. Best that I know," she said flatly.

"One man's meat is another man's poison. Same with women. Forget Roxanne and go with your gut feeling," he advised kindly, then gave her a crooked smile. "I can weather the storm in my department."

"Thanks, Graham." Her smile was wry. "Unfortunately, my experience tells me my gut feeling isn't wonderfully trustworthy."

"Up to you," he said with a shrug, and left her to mull over the madness that had consumed her last night.

Or was it madness?

She was older, wiser now than she'd been in the dizzy days of being swept along by Wayne's ardent courtship. Last night with Michael, she hadn't overlooked any false notes or responses that grated on her sense of harmony with him. There had been none. That was what had been so marvellous about everything. All those hours together and every minute of it sheer pleasure, once he had made up his mind to take a chance with her.

She could understand his wariness about associating with anyone at Global, apart from what his business necessitated. Global was Roxanne's stamping ground. Lauren acknowledged that she would certainly be reluctant to involve herself with anyone who worked with Wayne. Broken marriages did create conflict of interests areas.

It was little wonder he assumed a forbidding demeanour to anyone attached to Roxanne's milieu. No doubt he had only gone to Global's party out of friendship's sake, to provide company for Tasha Daniel while Evan gave his speech. Lauren had to respect him for that gesture alone. He couldn't have known beforehand that Roxanne wouldn't be there.

Though he did know she was not about to turn up after Beth Hayward had mentioned Roxanne's sprained ankle. Lauren remembered the sudden change in him, the casting aside of any inhibitions about showing he was attracted to her. Perhaps it was because the possible threat of Roxanne causing an unpleasant scene had been removed.

Lauren began to question Roxanne's version of her ex-husband's behaviour. Last night, when Michael had spoken of a saboteur, Lauren had assumed his ex-wife had taken a lover. If Roxanne had been unfaithful, there could be reason for him to demand an account of her time. Which had come first, the sense of oppression from Michael or the betrayal of his trust?

Lauren could well imagine Roxanne justifying her own behaviour by heaping blame on Michael. Probably the only way she could feel good about herself was by gaining sympathy for her course of action. When it came to the bottom line, Lauren readily conceded that Roxanne would never qualify as a bosom friend, whereas Michael could be the right man for her.

Hope dusted off the bleak desolation that had descended at Graham's revelation, but the bubble of undiluted happiness did not bounce back. A sense of caution kept it tightly confined. Despite her intense desire to dismiss all Roxanne's complaints against Michael, Lauren couldn't quite do it. The seeds of doubt had too much fertile ground to feed on from the hurts and disillusionment that had ended her own marriage.

She would give her gut feeling a chance to prove correct. After last night, it would be cowardly not to. Graham was right. She had to trust her own judgment. It wouldn't be fair to Michael otherwise.

Her telephone rang.

Satisfied she had sorted out her mind concerning Michael, Lauren focused her concentration on work as she picked up the receiver. "Lauren Magee," she said expectantly.

"Are you completely mad, Lauren?" Roxanne sounded peeved, pettish and sniping full bore.

"I beg your pardon." Some dousing dignity was called for.

"I can't believe you let Michael Timberlane sweep you off after all I've told you about him," Roxanne raged.

"I'm sorry. I've never heard you mention Michael Timberlane, Roxanne." And that was the cold, hard truth.

Silence. Some heavy breathing. "You didn't know he was my ex-husband?"

"How could I? We've never met before last night, and you always referred to your ex-husband as Mikey." Lauren screwed up her nose at the inappropriate little-boy name.

"Oh, my God! Did he know you didn't know?"

"I would think it was obvious. To me he was a perfect stranger." Maybe that had influenced his decision, too, knowing she wasn't prejudiced against him.

"Lauren, you didn't go to bed with him, did you?"

She bristled. "Aren't you being highly personal, Roxanne?"

"This *is* personal. He hates you, Lauren. Nothing would give him more satisfaction than to seduce you and have you begging for more."

A horrible chill crawled down Lauren's spine at the vehement conviction in Roxanne's voice.

"Why?" she asked brusquely. "Why should he hate me?"

"We used to have fights over what you said."

"What do you mean? I never said anything to him. I didn't know him."

"I mean when I threw your advice at him. He just couldn't take it. He started calling you the feminist saboteur in his sneering, superior way. Believe me, he hates you, Lauren. If you could have seen the savage look in his eyes whenever I brought up your name. Pure venom."

Shock didn't roll through Lauren's mind this time. It hit like jackhammer punches.

Feminist! Saboteur!

She felt sick. That was what had been going through Michael's mind during all that talk with Tasha and Evan. The savage flash in his eyes—it had been directed at her, not a memory. And once he realised Roxanne would not be coming to the party—the accident with the waiter, stopping Beth from blurting out his connection to Roxanne, was a very timely party trick, clearing the path to put his vengeful plan into action.

No, her heart screamed.

But it all added up.

"Look, I understand if he got to you," Roxanne went on. "He's a very sexy male animal when he decides to put out. But I'm warning you, Lauren. He'll turn on you as fast as look at you when it suits him. I hope you didn't let him have his rotten triumph over you."

Lauren gritted her teeth and swallowed the bile that had surged up her throat. "Triumph?" she repeated raggedly.

"He reckoned what you needed was a real man who'd knock all the feminist starch out of you and melt you into a human being. He would have gone all out to achieve that, and if he did..."

"I see. Well, thank you for calling, Roxanne," she managed stiffly and hung up, hating the thought that Michael might boast he had made her melt. Over and over again.

The perfect stranger. She should have realised he was too perfect to be real. Anyone could sustain an act for a night, especially if he knew what would strike a false note with her. Michael Timberlane was a highly intelligent man. He'd sucked her right in with his blend of sexiness and sensitivity to her desires and needs.

The telephone rang again. She hesitated, then berated herself for letting him affect her so deeply that she didn't want to take what might be an important call. Work was work, and it was far more reliable than people, she thought fiercely. At least she could count on herself to get it as right as she could in that area of her life. She picked up the receiver, but her voice was momentarily disconnected because of the miserable muddle in her mind.

"Lauren? It's Michael." Said with a soft lilt of anticipation.

Her stomach clenched. The arch-deceiver himself! If he thought she was about to rush in and beg for more, he could think again. "Yes?" she queried, her mind suddenly cold and clear.

"I found your note. It was a great night for me, too." Purring with pleasure.

"I'm glad it was mutual," she replied silkily, waiting for the perfect line to turn the knife.

He laughed. "Couldn't be more so. When do you think you'll finish work tonight?"

"Oh, I don't know. What do you want, Michael?" That was a good question. Let him beg!

"To be with you again as soon as you're free."

She deliberately heaved a sigh. "Look, Michael, it was a great night. A really great night. Let's leave it at that, shall we?"

Silence. "Come again?" He sounded puzzled, disbelieving.

Lauren went for the kill. "Well, the fact of the matter is I don't go in for repeat performances. Why spoil a perfect memory?"

"Performance?" he repeated harshly.

Got you, you rat!

"Mmm." It was the hum of satisfaction. She injected some warmth into her voice. Warm poison. "I've got to hand it to you, Michael. You certainly delivered. Thanks again. It was great."

She hung up to punctuate the finality of her farewell. And if that didn't turn the tables on his rotten triumph, she didn't know what would. A savage little smile curled her mouth. Vengeance could be sweet.

CHAPTER EIGHT

THEIR taxi was cruising towards Mascot. Lauren checked her watch. The flight to Melbourne was scheduled to leave at five. Domestic aircraft rarely departed on time. They would have a good twenty-five minutes to collect their tickets, check in their luggage, get their seat allocations and relax with a drink in the Golden Wing lounge.

It had been a long, exhausting day, racing between the ABC studios at Ultimo for the radio spots and the other venues for magazine interviews. Evan Daniel had performed well overall, gaining confidence and a dash of panache as he became more practised at handling the questions thrown at him. He was riding a high. Lauren felt totally limp.

It was as though last week's highly charged encounter with Michael Timberlane had drained something vital out of her. She wasn't sleeping well. Doing anything required a conscious effort. She forced herself to follow the schedules she set, but somehow she couldn't lift herself out of this . . . this slough of despondency. Sometimes she even wished she was dead.

The taxi was beetling along, the driver seemingly unconcerned that the cars in front of him were stopped at a red traffic light. Did he expect it to

change? Alarm shot through Lauren's nerves.
Couldn't he see?

"I say," Evan started weakly.

Lauren screamed.

The driver snapped alert, slammed on the brakes
and the tyres burnt rubber to a squealing halt, mil-
limetres from the stationary traffic ahead of them.
Brakes shrieked from the car behind them as it nar-
rowly avoided crashing into the back of the taxi.

"Sorry," their driver mumbled.

Evan turned from the front seat to check on
Lauren. "Are you okay?"

"Yes," she replied shakily, then with a dark look
at the back of their driver's head, added, "I would
like to get to the airport in one piece though."

"I think I need a double gin," Evan said with
feeling.

It didn't sound like a bad idea to Lauren, either,
although the adrenaline kick of the near accident
had proved one thing to her. She definitely didn't
want to be dead. There was life after inattentive
taxidrivers and Michael Timberlane. It was up to
her to make the best of it. And she would.
Somehow.

It had only been a week since the disastrous
morning after. Perhaps she had been subconscious-
ly grieving a lost dream. This trip to Melbourne
should lift her spirits. Tonight she would visit her
mother and whatever family was at home. It was
always heart-warming to be with people whom she
cared about and who cared about her. Lauren didn't

want anything to do with hatred. It was a destructive emotion.

It was a relief to leave the errant taxi and enter the bustle of the terminal. Here were people on the move, going somewhere, doing something, excitement, adventure, change... Lauren loved the mood of airports. The check-in went smoothly, and anticipation began to tingle through her as they rode the escalator up to the waiting areas. She was flying home.

The Golden Wing lounge seemed packed when they entered. "I'll look for some seats while you get your drink, Evan," Lauren offered.

"No problem. Michael should have bagged a table somewhere."

"Michael?" Her heart fluttered.

"Ah, there he is!" Evan said with satisfaction, pointing to a window table across the room from the bar.

Lauren's heart dropped to the floor. The dark, striking figure of Michael Timberlane, lounging at ease, idly perusing a business magazine, burned through her retinas and stamped itself on her quivering mind. Her peripheral vision took in the two chairs grouped with his, one occupied by a flight bag, the other by a newspaper. He was expecting them, waiting for them.

Goosebumps broke out on Lauren's skin. She wasn't finished with him. He wasn't going to let her be finished with him. Just like Wayne. He had his own agenda, and to hell with what she wanted!

Rebellion stirred, pumping her heart into its rightful place. If Michael Timberlane thought he could get at her again, he was in for a big surprise. The trick was to act as though this meeting was totally inconsequential to her. Which it was. She would get that message across to him if it killed her.

She forced her legs to follow Evan as he picked his way towards his friend. *Head high,* she advised herself, and fiercely wished she'd pinned her hair up this morning. It was wildly afloat around her shoulders, and Michael had made almost a fetish of it in their lovemaking. Such a reminder was unwelcome, but it had to be borne with an air of carelessness.

She was glad she was wearing a tailored slacks suit. If Michael Timberlane wanted to make something feminist of that, let him. At least it didn't mould her body in any overt way, not even with the jacket off. She had added a jazzy little vest featuring white reindeers on bands of mustard and black, and it neatly skimmed the curves her black skivvy and slacks would have outlined. Except for her hair, she presented a smartly professional appearance.

"We got here!" Evan announced, alerting Michael to their arrival. "No thanks to the taxi driver who gave us one hell of a fright."

"Oh?" Michael queried as he put his magazine aside and rose to his feet, looking sleek, dangerous and disturbingly virile in blue jeans and a black leather jacket.

"If Lauren hadn't screamed, I reckon we would have crashed for sure," Evan went on with the relish of a storyteller.

A sardonic smile was directed at her. "I congratulate you on your timely screaming, Lauren."

"It took siren strength to wake the driver," she said, jollying the story along, pretending his presence had no import to her.

His silvery eyes swept a glittering glance over her hair, then shot piercing derision at her as he observed, "When it comes to siren quality, you certainly have it in quantity."

So the knives were out, Lauren thought. No intent to seduce again. This was counter-kill time. Which suited her just fine. Where Michael Timberlane was concerned, she was armour-plated.

She smiled at Evan. "If you're going to have a drink..."

"You bet I am." He grinned and patted his stomach. "Needs some settling down. What will you have, Lauren? You can fill Michael in on our drama while I get our medicinal measures."

"A lemon squash will be fine for me."

"You're joking!"

"No. I find alcohol drying on flights."

"There's an easy solution to that. Drink more." Evan advised.

She shook her head. No way was she going to fuzz her brain in the present circumstances. If she'd drunk less champagne the last time she was with Michael Timberlane, she might not have lost her head in a cloud of rosy dreams.

"Lemon squash," Evan conceded with mock disgust. "What can I get you, Michael?"

"I'll join you in a gin."

"Double?"

"Why not?"

Evan grinned at the ready camaraderie from his friend. "A Waki special coming up," he promised and headed to the bar.

Michael leaned over and lifted the flight bag off the chair opposite his. "Have a seat," he invited.

"Thank you."

It was a comfortable tub chair, and Lauren deliberately struck a relaxed pose, settling back against the cushioned upholstery, laying her arms openly on the armrests and crossing her legs. If Michael Timberlane was adept at reading body language, the message she was projecting was as easygoing as she could get. Lauren was not about to show him any sign of tension.

He adopted a more casual posture, elbows on the armrests, hands dangling loosely, one foot resting on the other knee. He surveyed her slowly from head to toe, a deliberate stripping, meant to shame and unsettle her. Lauren wished she could do the same to him but found she couldn't carry it off.

The blue chambray shirt he wore was open-necked. When her eyes hit the springy black curls nesting below the base of his throat, the memory of their intimacy was triggered too forcefully. She didn't want to face it. She turned her gaze to the window and looked at the aircraft lined up at their boarding tunnels. Baggage was being loaded into the closest one. Watching that process was pleasantly mind-numbing.

"Do you have business in Melbourne?" she asked when it became obvious he did not intend offering any conversation. If he had some battle plan against her she preferred some warning of what to expect.

Silence.

She directed a look of polite enquiry at him, determined to show his rudeness did not affect her.

"No," he answered, a mocking challenge in his eyes.

"But you are flying with us," she persisted, wanting at least the present situation clarified.

"Yes, I'm coming along for the ride."

"Why?"

"I guess you could say I'm riding shotgun for Evan and Tasha."

She frowned. "You think they need protecting?"

"Yes. You may consider it rather quaint of me, but I care about them. They're meaningful people in my life. And God knows I've found few enough of them."

The sarcasm cut. It was difficult to ignore. "Who would want to hurt them?" she asked. None of the interviews she had lined up were in the go-for-the-jugular category. It was all human-interest fare; easy, informative, entertaining.

"You."

"Me?" She stared incredulously at him.

"Don't come the innocent, Lauren," he said harshly, his eyes flashing contempt. "I've been there with you and know what's at the end of it. If Evan is chalked up as your next dalliance, I aim to prevent it.''

Hatred, hard and violent, coming at her in heart-jolting, throat-constricting, mind-jamming waves. Lauren had never been subjected to anything like it before. For several moments she could do nothing but sit in mesmerised horror at what had been wrought in him by her act of vengeance.

She collected herself with difficulty. He hated her before she even met him, she reasoned. He deserved everything she had handed out for having played so falsely with her. There was no cause for guilt or shame on her part.

Nevertheless, it was frightening that her ego wounding had fired his hatred to such a high level of intensity. Would he do her harm if he got the chance? More harm than he had already done with *his* act of vengeance? Had he poisoned Evan's mind against her?

No. The answer was swift and certain. Evan was treating her no differently. His personality was too open to cover up any harbouring of ill will towards her. There had been no confidences. This was a private thing, a deep festering of wounds that cut to the innermost core of Michael Timberlane.

"I don't dally with married men," she stated flatly, wanting at least that part of his picture of her corrected.

"What a nice distinction." Pure acid. "If true."

She shrugged. "Believe what you like, Michael." Her mouth twisted with irony. "You will, anyway."

"I keep thinking of your poor sucker of a husband. No wonder he didn't like your job," he drawled. "All those convenient hotel rooms and a quick change of authors to provide variety. How many notches have you got on your belt, Lauren?"

He was so far off beam she could let his offensiveness float over her. She raised a taunting eyebrow. "Hurt pride, Michael?"

"Curiosity." His thin-lipped smile deflected the hit. "As a specimen of the modern female, you're quite an interesting study, Lauren."

"I do hope you're open-minded enough to take response to stimuli into consideration," she said sweetly. "You were—" she fluttered her gaze from his chest to his thighs in a deliberate parody of his sexual survey "—very stimulating."

She saw the powerful leg muscles tauten against the stretch denim of his jeans and felt a savage triumph at having affected him, despite his contemptuous attitude towards her.

"But you prefer a change of flesh," he said, rushing to the worst judgment again.

She raised her gaze, subjecting him to a mocking challenge. "Do I? Leaping to conclusions from faulty assumptions does not strike me as a sound way of conducting a study. Where's your body of evidence, Michael?"

His mouth curled. "You gave it to me, Lauren."

She forced a tinkling laugh. "How marvellous it must be to confidently extract the pattern of a person's life from one incident."

"Hardly an incident," he drawled. "More a revelation."

"Indeed?"

His deceit burned through her, igniting energy resources that had lain dormant for days. One thing could be said for Michael Timberlane's unwelcome intrusion in her life again. He generated an electricity that had her firing on all cylinders.

She leaned forward and gave him an earnestly questioning look. "Could there possibly be a vital piece of the picture missing? Something critical that the genius has overlooked in his summing up?"

His eyes narrowed.

She flopped back in her chair in careless dismissal of whatever answers he came up with, scorning his arrogance in judging her so meanly when the mean-heartedness was all his.

He leaned forward, his eyes hypnotically luminescent in their need to know. "Enlighten me, Lauren. Tell me the missing factor."

"You don't recall the factor you so deliberately left out of the equation, Michael?" she tossed at him. She couldn't quite keep the contempt out of her voice as she added, "Neat trick with the drink waiter. Very timely."

He reeled, face tightening as though she had slapped him. He shook his head. His mouth thinned. Another more vehement shake of the head. With a startling burst of explosive energy, he jack-knifed forward, his eyes riveting hers in a blaze of sizzling emotion.

"Are you telling me you let Roxanne influence you?" It was a blistering hiss. "After what we shared?"

She felt the memories if that night pulsing from him, bombarding her mind, curling around her heart, squeezing it. And the thought came to her that hatred was the reverse side of love ... love betrayed, belittled, abused. Had she leapt to all the wrong conclusions?

Lauren was so paralysed by this appalling possibility she could make no response. Inwardly she retreated from the assault of his eyes, closing up, guarding herself from making any further mistakes. Confusion, emotional turbulence, a deep, dark sickness in her soul.

"Here we are!"

Three glasses clinked onto the table. Evan Daniel back from the bar, a lemon squash for her, double gins for the men. She wished she'd ordered something with the kick of a mule. It might have anaesthetised the painful chaos of trying to evaluate where she was and what she should do about Michael Timberlane.

"Thanks, Evan," he said, picking up his glass, composing himself in a flash. He smiled at his friend, master of himself, master of the situation, and lifted his glass in a toast. "You did yourself and your book proud today."

"You listened to the radio spots?" Evan's grin was pure delight.

"With keen attention. You warmed up very nicely. Tomorrow should be a breeze for you."

His comments echoed Lauren's assessment of Evan's performance, reminding her how closely in tune they had seemed to be, the sense of real sharing. It gave her a hollow feeling, knowing she had rejected it all. What if there had been no mal-evolent intent to deceive and seduce?

She picked up her glass, sipping the sharp tangy drink while Evan rehashed the interviews, inviting Michael's opinion on various aspects of them. It was obvious he valued and respected Michael's judgment, hanging on his words as though they were pure gold.

No gold for her, though, Lauren caustically re-minded herself. His judgments where she was con-cerned had been downright nasty, making her out to be a promiscuous siren, luring men to her bed for one-night stands. And that totally uncalled for crack about her husband being a poor sucker... Lauren gritted her teeth in bitter resentment. What right did he have to paint her so black? He knew nothing, absolutely nothing about her marriage!

On the other side of the ledger, she didn't really know what had gone on in his marriage. She only had Roxanne's word for how he had behaved, what he had thought and felt and said. Graham Parker was sceptical of Roxanne's version of the truth, yet what she had told Lauren about Michael's attitude towards her struck a few truths with Lauren.

His quickness to make harsh judgments was not a trait that endeared him to her, no matter that she had given him some cause to think badly of her. He had jumped right in and thought the worst. No benefit of the doubt. No pause for reflection. No wondering if he had done something wrong.

Lauren didn't need that.

Destructive.

She'd been through one destructive relationship. She certainly didn't need another. She wanted... how that one night with Michael had been. But he'd shown her the other side of the coin of love, the blind passion of hatred.

A shudder ran through her.

As though his sensory perception was acutely tuned to her, Michael snapped his attention from Evan, his laser eyes sweeping Lauren like searchlights, determined on pinpointing what she was feeling and thinking.

No. No more, she thought.

The memory was spoiled.

Irrevocably.

"Ansett Flight AN37 is boarding now. Would passengers please proceed to the departure lounge?"

Lauren set her glass down and stood. She was going home. The only person she wanted right now was her mother.

CHAPTER NINE

REGRETS savaged Michael's stomach as they moved out of the Golden Wing lounge. Roxanne! His teeth gritted at the name. So many times during that magical night with Lauren the warning had rung in his mind—*Tell her now. Tell her about Roxanne.* And he had put off doing it because he hadn't wanted to break the incredibly exhilarating and soul-lifting rapport flowing between them.

And that critical piece of communication had become less and less important as the night wore on. Their intimacy had been too precious, too intensely felt to admit any third party. To have introduced the subject of Roxanne would have been crass. It could be done in the morning before Lauren left, he had told himself.

If only he hadn't slept on.

If only Lauren had woken him before going.

Yet would he have told her?

If he was ruthlessly honest with himself, the answer was almost certainly no. Roxanne had become totally irrelevant, lost in the wonder of all Lauren promised. He hadn't even given her a fleeting thought when he had rung Global that morning, eager to speak to Lauren, ebullient with a happiness so intense and pervasive there hadn't been room for any thought but renewing the link with Lauren.

A link that had already been broken.

A link he had just comprehensively smashed, probably beyond repair, in his bitter attack on her supposed lack of morality and callous using of people.

He didn't have to look at Lauren to know how effective he'd been in destroying the special bond they had shared. The three of them were heading towards the departure lounge together, but they weren't together. She walked with them but apart. Michael keenly felt the separation.

He'd seen the decision crystallise in her eyes, the vulnerable bright blue of cornflowers hardening, glinting into the cold, hard surface of sapphires, shutting him out. The walls were up, forbidding any entry to her space. She walked alone.

And it was all his own damned fault! No, not all. His precious ex-wife had a few things to answer for. Couldn't keep her nose out of his business despite having bagged a husband who pandered to her self-centred little soul. But, of course, the idea of him and Lauren together wouldn't sit well with her, not after all she'd said about both of them. It would show her up for the shallow, selfish, two-faced person she was.

God! Couldn't Lauren see that?

They turned into the nominated departure lounge, he and Evan automatically hanging back for Lauren to hand in her boarding pass first. She went ahead without demur. No feminist stand about equality when it came to traditional courtesy. There rarely was, Michael reflected. Not that he classed Lauren as a rabid feminist anymore. She was an intelligent woman who wanted her intelligence respected. Nothing extreme in that attitude.

She picked up a packet of headphones on her way into the boarding tunnel. It was an ominous sign. Headphones would provide a communication block during the flight. He needed to talk to her, needed to get things straightened out between them, needed to apologise for the rotten things he'd said. And thought. And done.

His gaze was drawn to the sensual undulation of her buttocks as her long legs put more distance between them on the short walk along the tunnel to the aircraft. He could feel the imprint of their softly cushioned roundness pressed against his groin in the aftermath of lovemaking. It reawakened the wanting that had hit him the moment he had seen her again. He wrenched his eyes up, but the vibrant bounce of her glorious hair made the ache of desire worse.

Damn, damn, damn! he could feel himself bulging, stretching the crotch of his jeans. *Think cold*, he commanded. If he couldn't match Lauren's coolness, he was a dead man. He was probably dead anyway. At the present moment, he doubted she would touch him with a barge pole. How he was going to recapture what he'd lost he didn't know, but he had to start somewhere and he'd better get it right.

The stewardess smiled a greeting, her eyes sparking female interest at him. It irritated him. Unreasonably. Hadn't he been instantly and strongly affected by Lauren's physical attractions? Still was. Yet what was inside her head and heart was far more important to him. And more than anything he wanted a woman who could see and share what was in his head and heart. With honesty. Not the pretence Roxanne had given him in the beginning.

Lauren. Her openness had delighted him, enthralled him, entranced him. He followed her down the aisle the stewardess directed them to, determined to break through the barriers that now shut him out. Lauren Magee was the woman he craved in every sense there was... his other half. Or certainly the closest he'd ever come to it. He had to win her back.

She stopped by two vacant seats on the window side. A third vacant seat was directly across the aisle in the middle section of the plane. She looked at it and Michael knew it would be her choice if he didn't do some fast manoeuvring.

"There's some space in the overhead lockers a bit further along, Lauren," he directed.

She glanced up and moved, intent on storing her briefcase and jacket out of the way.

Michael turned to Evan who was behind him. "Better take this seat," he advised, steering him straight into it. "Easier to catch the drink waiter's eye right here on the aisle."

Evan cheerfully obliged. Lauren cast a sharp look over her shoulder, saw the fait accompli, and without a word proceeded to stow her excess belongings into a locker. Michael jammed his flight bag in beside them, then backtracked to allow her to move in to the window seat ahead of him.

She stopped by Evan. "The view over Sydney is so lovely, like a fairyland with all the lights on, Evan," she said persuasively. "You really should take the window seat. I've seen it dozens of times. Besides, if I sit here, you'll be seated right next to Michael and can talk to him more easily."

Evan clearly wavered for a moment. Then he had the good sense to look at Michael and get the message in no uncertain terms. "No, no, I'm fine here," he declared, waving magnanimously as he added, "You and Michael sit together."

Done! And she knew it was done. She didn't bother to argue. With a nod of compliance she moved to the seat allocated to her by Michael, but if she felt trapped by the situation he had engineered, she didn't show it. Not a hint of frustration, vexation, resignation or surrender. She sat down with an air of insular dignity, fastened her seat belt, folded her hands in her lap and turned her face to the window.

He settled beside her.

She ignored his presence as steadfastly as though he didn't exist.

He had to strike now, Michael decided, before she put the headphones on and blocked her hearing.

"I apologise," he said, his voice low, throbbing with sincerity.

There was no indication she had heard. She remained wrapped in stillness, her face obscured by her hair so he couldn't see if there was some change of expression on it. He stared at her hands, their long elegant fingers quiescent, as withdrawn from him as the rest of her. They could be part of a marble statue, he thought, so white and lifeless, yet the memory of their warm, erotic touch set his skin tingling with the want and need to feel it again.

"What for?"

Flat words, disembodied, ejected without any physical accompaniment to reflect that she had spoken them, but they were a response. Michael's mind went into a spin, like a roulette wheel bouncing the ball around until it stopped at what he hoped was a winning number.

"For not trusting what I'd felt with you."

That was the core of it. She hadn't trusted it, either, letting Roxanne colour her natural response to him, cutting him off without even granting him a fair hearing. A sense of injustice welled up, rekindling the frustration and fury that had fed the false image she had given him in brushing him off like the used mate of a black widow spider after she'd devoured all she wanted of him.

How could she have been so ruthless, so destructive? On the spurious strength of Roxanne's self-serving view of him? Michael was working himself up to a fine sense of justification when

Lauren spoke, shattering any feeling of self-righteousness.

"You judged." Hard, implacable words, delivered without inflexion, without a trace of bending movement.

He heard the black hood of condemnation in her voice, felt the sentence of death hovering over him and instantly fought it. "You did, too, Lauren."

A slight shake of the head. Slowly she turned to look at him. Sapphire eyes. No quarter given. "I let it go, Michael. No rancour, no nastiness, no coming after you with guns blazing."

Guilty heat burned across his cheekbones. He'd wanted to reduce her to nothing. She'd left him feeling like nothing. But he'd had no real evidence to suggest she might play dirty with Evan. Or that she'd ever been unfaithful to her husband. That had been pure bile on his part, pumped out of the turbulent feelings she stirred with her apparent indifference to him.

"I'm sorry. What I said was unwarranted and undeserved," he acknowledged.

"Yes, it was. It's indicative of what I can expect from you if your desires are thwarted," she coolly added.

"No." The glittering scepticism in her eyes urged him to more vehement emphasis. "I swear it won't be like that. I know better now."

The scepticism didn't waver. "I'm sorry. I won't take that risk. Just let it go, Michael. Gracefully."

She turned away and stared out the window again.

Everything in Michael rebelled against her edict. Before he could think of any effective argument against it, the in-flight intercom came on, announcing imminent departure. The stewardesses directed attention to the television screens showing the usual safety procedures in the event of various mishaps occurring. The advice floated over Michael's head. He was facing death of a different kind, and all his concentration was bent on changing the path of his future.

As the aircraft taxied towards its take-off runway he struggled with the most compelling urge to reach across and grasp Lauren's hand, forcing a physical link between them. Yet she might interpret it as an aggressive act, overriding her wishes. Which it was. But if it recalled and reinforced the intimacy they had known together, might it not weaken the reservations she had against him? Would touch achieve what words could not?

The last resort, he sternly told himself. He was not under extreme time pressure. If he couldn't break through to Lauren this evening, he still had tomorrow. He would make plenty of opportunities to wear down the rigid barriers she had erected. Each moment spent with her would be an information-gathering exercise. Sooner or later he would find the key that would open her door again. In the meantime, he had to appear to respect her wishes.

The aircraft gathered speed and lifted off. The stewardess came by taking drink orders. She provided Michael with a legitimate and inoffensive reason to draw Lauren's attention away from the window.

"Lauren, the stewardess is asking about drinks," he said matter-of-factly.

She turned her head, her gaze shooting straight past him. "Nothing for me, thank you."

So much for a companionable drink, Michael thought, and echoed Evan's order of a gin and tonic for himself. He needed something to occupy his hands and keep them out of temptation, and gin did soothe the beast inside him.

Lauren started tearing open the pocket containing the headphones.

"Is conversation with me anathema to you?" he asked.

She paused and lifted a wary gaze to his.

He gave her an appealing smile. "I promise to be civilised."

"It won't do any good, Michael," she said quickly. "We're each carrying baggage that won't go away."

His smile turned rueful. "Are you referring to Roxanne?"

"Amongst other things."

"I assure you Roxanne is totally expunged from my life."

Her eyes derided his assertion. "Feminist, saboteur, hatred..." A succinct list, delivered with deadly aim.

"I threw away that load before I bumped the drink waiter's arm at the party."

"Deceit," she added, shooting at his integrity.

"I didn't tell you about Roxanne because I wanted what happened between us to be free of prejudice. Was that unreasonable, Lauren?"

"It was wrong not to give me a choice. You chose, Michael. You should have trusted me to choose, too."

He couldn't answer that. Excuses were useless. She had cut straight to the heart of the matter and laid it bare for him.

"You see?" Her smile was a wry twist. "You judged. You did what suited you. And I'm sure you'll justify it. Men like you always do."

"Men like me?"

"That's my baggage, Michael." Her eyes had changed again. Bleak winter blue, dull and flat. "Now, if you'll excuse me, I'm very tired. I don't want any refreshments."

She put the headphones on, plugged into the sound system, relaxed in her seat and closed her eyes. He let it go . . . for now. She'd given him a lot to think about.

His mind circled around honesty and trust. It was what he wanted in a relationship. Lauren was right in saying he had denied her that. And he had justified it. He could see how wrong he had been not to let her know about Roxanne straightaway, giving her a fair chance to make up her own mind about him. He had played to his own advantage.

However, she was wrong in thinking he would keep justifying it. He was not in the habit of repeating mistakes once he had been shown where he had erred.

Doing what suited him... Roxanne would have fed that line to Lauren until she was brainwashed with it. Roxanne twisted everything around to suit herself. It wasn't true of him. Or was it?

Leaving Roxanne and her lies out of consideration, how had he come across to Lauren?

It had suited him not to reveal that Roxanne was his ex-wife. It had suited him to come on this trip. He had used the excuse of protecting Evan and Tasha, but the real reason was he wanted to face Lauren with what she had rejected. It had suited him to manoeuvre her into the window seat. Selfish and self-serving. That was the truth of it.

Yet the memory of their night together was the driving force behind his pursuit of her, and it wasn't only his future happiness at stake. Lauren had been just as committed to total involvement. He had to convince her it wasn't a mistake, for both their sakes. He had to prove he wasn't like the men she was comparing him to in her mind.

How many other men, he wondered?

Her ex-husband for a start. Something must have gone badly wrong there. The others were probably irrelevant, he decided. Her marriage would have been the crucible that had cemented her attitude towards what she did and did not want in a man. His marriage had certainly sorted him out about what was important to him and what wasn't.

Tasha's recipe for a happy marriage slid into his mind. *It's wanting the same things.*

He looked at Lauren. Did she want what he wanted? Her magnificent hair frothed around the constriction of the headphones. Her profile in repose had a purity of line and proportion that would have appealed to any artist. There was a translucence to her pale skin, giving an impression of fragility. Under the sweep of her lashes lay shadows he hadn't noticed when her eyes were open. The result of sleepless nights? Had she lain awake, mourning the despoiling of a dream?

He wished he could cradle her in his arms, wished they could go back a week and start again. He gathered every shred of willpower he had and drove it into a telepathic message.

Give me another chance, Lauren. That's all I ask. Another chance.

CHAPTER TEN

"THE Como Hotel, Chapel Street, South Yarra," Lauren said to the taxidriver, hoping he was capable of giving them a problem-free trip.

"Going to be slow, I'm afraid," he informed them cheerfully. "Lot of traffic tonight. Big rugby league match on at the MCG."

"Of course. Queensland against New South Wales in the second of the State of Origin matches," Evan cried, his face lighting up with eager interest. "What's the betting here in Melbourne?"

"The money's on New South Wales, but most people I talk to want Queensland to win." The driver grinned. "Sorry if that's against your home state, but that's how it is."

They chatted on about state rivalries as the driver stowed their luggage in the boot of the taxi. Michael, she noted, did not join in the conversation. He moved around to the far passenger side, leaving her and Evan to take their places in the car wherever they willed. No direction from him this time. Had he let go? Given up?

She frowned, knowing it was positively perverse of her to feel disappointed. If he was respecting her decision, she should be approving his restraint, glad to be relieved of the stress involved in resisting continual pressure to change her mind. Best to make a clean break of it. Perhaps he saw it was the wisest course, too.

Lauren hesitated over whether to sit in the front or the back of the taxi. It was easier for Evan to carry on his football chat with the driver if he sat beside him. It didn't really matter where she sat. Michael Timberlane would still be sharing the same space as herself, and she wouldn't escape being aware of him. Even with her eyes shut and music playing in her ears on the flight to Melbourne, she had been unable to block him out.

Michael was already settled on the back seat when she chose to join him. His eyes flashed with surprise, then kindled with warm pleasure. His mouth curved into a slow, teasing little smile that somehow expressed both hope and self-mockery.

"Does this mean my sins are forgiven?"

The smile and the soft lilt of his voice played havoc with her composure. The corners of her mouth twitched. Her sense of fun wanted release. It was difficult to control the impulse to respond in kind, to let her eyes flirt with his. *Remember, remember how quickly he can change,* she sternly berated herself. It was incredibly stupid of her to suddenly feel light-hearted, pleased that he hadn't given up.

"I think that's between you and God," she answered blandly. "Isn't hatred one of the seven deadly sins?"

"No. Pride, avarice, lust, anger, gluttony, envy and sloth," he answered, with admirable recall of that rather arcane piece of knowledge. His eyebrows slanted in comic ruefulness. "You've definitely got me on three of them, and I've been in sackcloth and ashes all the way from Sydney, doing penance."

Lauren was having real difficulty in keeping her mouth straight. As an exercise in self-control she did a mental juggle and came up with pride, lust and anger for the three deadly sins he confessed to. Lauren was highly unsettled by the fact she was having considerable trouble with lust herself.

Despite her serious reservations about Michael Timberlane's character, she could barely glance at him without remembering and wanting the sexual excitement and intense pleasure of his lovemaking. His mouth was sinfully sensual, the smile playing on it extremely provocative, suggesting soft and tantalising little movements.

She wrenched her eyes away from the inviting twinkle in his and glanced out the rear window, where Evan and the taxidriver were nattering away, taking their time about getting going. She wished they'd hurry up. Michael Timberlane was far too treacherously attractive for any peace of mind.

How many times had she excused inexcusable things from Wayne for the comforting illusion of closeness that physical intimacy provided? If she didn't apply the lessons learnt from painful experience, she was a fool. Sexual attraction—lust—was treacherous. One didn't spend one's whole life in bed. There had to be something good in the rest of it.

"Did Roxanne say I hated you?" Michael asked quietly.

"Yes." And she'd better keep remembering that, too.

"I've never hated anyone, Lauren."

The sweeping claim was such a downright lie, it swung her gaze to his in sizzling challenge.

"I confess I was fed up with hearing 'Lauren says' every time Roxanne wanted to score off me, but my hatred was for the way she wouldn't face up to—"

"I'm not stupid, Michael," Lauren cut in impatiently. "I know what I felt coming from you in the Golden Wing lounge."

His expression instantly changed, responding to the seriousness of the charge. He nodded gravely. "Yes, that was hatred, Lauren. The hatred of knowing the guts had been torn out of something I believed beautiful and seeing the shell of it still there, yet unable to fix it, unable to breathe life into it again."

His eyes stabbed into hers, tearing at her interpretation of his emotions. "I certainly hated that. I can't view the destruction of something rare and precious with indifference or even equanimity."

The passion emanating from him, throbbing through his voice and flashing from his eyes, clutched at her heart and shook her mind into encompassing more than it had before. Rare and precious. She had felt that, too.

"I hate a lot of things people do and say, especially when it hurts others," he went on. "And now I find I'm guilty of that myself, much as I regret it.'' He heaved a sigh. His eyes softened to appeal. "Hasn't there ever been a time when you wish you could undo what you've done and make it better?''

Lauren felt so churned around it was a welcome relief when their private tête-à-tête was broken by Evan and the taxidriver, finally taking their seats. Football talk flowed unabated from the front of the cab as the taxi left Tullamarine Airport and headed for the city. The good-natured banter provided a convenient cover for Lauren's retreat into herself.

Her thoughts were turbulent. The straight line she had drawn in her mind was now wavering all over the place. Michael had pleaded a strong case for himself. Everybody made mistakes. While never having set out to hurt anyone, Lauren had her own private list of things she'd do differently, given the time again. It was all too easy to jump in and make black-and-white judgments instead of waiting to weigh all sides of a situation.

Maybe she should give him another chance.

If it hadn't been for Roxanne feeding her the hate message... Had that been inspired by what Graham Parker predicted would be a dog-in-the-manger attitude? Roxanne could hardly call her second husband a sexy male animal. He was close to fifty, carried a middle-aged paunch and somehow reminded Lauren of a lolloping lick-happy Labrador. Whereas Michael had the sleek, beautiful, lethal power of a Doberman.

Her gaze strayed sideways. His hand rested loosely on his thigh. She knew the tensile strength of those muscle-moulded legs, knew the tenderness and sensual skill of his hands. There wasn't one part of his magnificent body that she didn't know intimately, the way it felt, the way it responded to her, the way it could make her feel.

She could picture it perfectly, remember the exquisite sensations... A purely wanton excitement coursed through her, tightening her muscles. If she reached out to him...

Lauren took a deep breath and clamped down on the dangerous impulse. She wasn't prepared to commit herself so wholly to Michael Timberlane again, not until she was more sure of what he was really like. She needed to see how he reacted to a number of situations before giving him her complete trust. Another chance didn't mean shutting her eyes and hoping for the best.

She looked out the side window to keep temptation at bay. The taxidriver was right about the traffic. It was crawling from one red light to the next.

"We'll be out of this at the next turn right," he announced in his genial manner. "We should have a better run to your hotel from there."

A few moments later he manoeuvred the taxi into the right-hand turning lane, and there they stopped, waiting for another light to change. The stream of cars on Lauren's side kept flowing for a while, then came to a halt, as well. She admired the stylish line of the electric blue sports car that had drawn level

with the taxi. It stirred a curiosity about its owner.
She glanced at the driver and gasped in shock.

Wayne!

She stared disbelievingly at his profile, trying to
convince herself it must be a look-alike. There were
other men with curly black hair, aquiline noses and
full-lipped mouths. Wayne wouldn't waste his
money on an expensive sports car. It couldn't be
him. It was too much of a coincidence, seeing her
ex-husband like this when he had been featuring so
much in her thoughts about Michael.

As though sensing he was being stared at, the
object of her inner turmoil suddenly turned his head
and looked straight at her. A steel clamp squeezed
her heart. It *was* Wayne! And his recognition of
her was instant and frightening.

His dark eyes glittered as they always did when
he won his way about something. His mouth curled
with satisfaction. She was here in Melbourne, and
he knew she was here. Despite the length of time
they had been apart, there was no resigned acceptance of their separation, for Wayne.

Lauren silently and fiercely railed against the
fickle trick of fate that had placed them both here.
Two years had passed since she had broken with
him. She had taken care that their paths didn't
cross. Avoidance at all costs had been her strategy
for a trouble-free life. Now this, of all times and
all places!

Wayne leaned forward to look at the man sitting
beside her in the back seat. Was Michael aware of
it? Was he watching? She dared not glance at him.

It would reinforce the kind of personal connection she didn't want Wayne to make. Though surely with Evan in the front seat, Wayne would realise it was a business trip and not a private outing.

She saw his jaw tighten into pugnacious mode. He glared at her, angry, jealous, possessive. His attitudes certainly hadn't changed. The sports car was probably an ego-booster, another superficial attraction to add to his pulling power with women, but however many women there had been in his life since her departure, he still resented her leaving him. A wife didn't do that, in Wayne's world. A wife did as she was told and pleased her husband.

The taxi started moving forward. Wayne jerked his attention to the cars ahead of him. They were also on the move, and since they were not in a turning lane there was nothing to slow them down. Wayne drew level again, threw her one last baleful glare, then, prompted by a horn blowing behind him, accelerated away.

Lauren wasn't really aware of the rest of the drive to the hotel. Memories of her marriage to Wayne crowded in on her. She became conscious, at one point, of her fingernails digging into her palms. Her hands were tightly clenched. She uncurled them and stretched out her fingers.

No mark remained on the third finger of her left hand. When she had walked out on Wayne, she had left the rings he had given her behind, too. They should have been symbols of belonging together, not domination.

"Are you all right, Lauren?" Michael asked softly.

She swung around to face him, instinctively defying his concern, not wanting to discuss what she was feeling and why. "Yes, of course. Why wouldn't I be?"

His eyes probed hers but met a blank wall. "You didn't eat on the flight," he remarked. "The hotel restaurant, Maxim's, has an excellent reputation. Evan and I plan to have a leisurely dinner there. If you're not too tired, we'd both like your company."

A tactically worded invitation, designed to allay any fears that he might come on to her. In the normal course of events she might have accepted. Nothing was normal now.

"Thank you, but I won't join you."

He frowned. "Because of me?"

She shook her head. "My family live in Melbourne. I'm going to visit my mother."

"Fair enough."

Lauren didn't care if it was fair or not. Michael Timberlane could wait. She didn't want any man close to her right now. She needed her mother, her sane, sensible, down-to-earth mother, who was never flustered by anything.

They arrived at the Como Hotel. It was situated right next to the Channel Ten studios and catered to the security concerns of visiting celebrities. Lauren was glad of the security measures that protected all the guests from unwanted visitors. No one could operate an elevator without a room key. Once they were booked in and on their way to their rooms, she would feel safe from Wayne.

She kept an eye on the road while the luggage was unloaded, and she got a receipt from the driver for the taxi fare. No electric blue sports car pulled up or cruised by. Her apprehension eased somewhat as they proceeded inside to the reception desk.

When she was absolutely certain Wayne hadn't tracked her to the hotel, she would ask the concierge to have a taxi waiting at the door for her and she would slip out of the hotel and go home. That took care of tonight.

Tomorrow... Well, she would cope with tomorrow as best she could when it came.

CHAPTER ELEVEN

NO WONDER Evan was overweight, Michael reflected, idly watching him heap strawberry conserve onto his third piece of toast. This followed a cooked breakfast comprising eggs, bacon, grilled tomato and hash browns, which had been preceded by a bowl of muesli heaped with dried fruit. However, it could be argued that Evan would burn up a lot of energy today with the list of interviews Lauren had lined up for him.

She hadn't come down to the restaurant for breakfast. Not yet, anyway. Michael checked his watch. Evan was to meet her in the foyer at nine-thirty. It was now eight twenty-six. Still time for her to appear. On the other hand, perhaps she preferred to eat in her room. Or was she deliberately avoiding him?

"We've plenty of time, haven't we?" Evan asked.

"Yes. I think I might have some cheese with my coffee."

Michael stood up to go to the continental breakfast smorgasbord. The glass frontage of the restaurant faced the reception area. He caught sight of Lauren hurrying down the half flight of steps from the foyer. In the few seconds it took her to race through reception to the elevators, Michael was struck by far more than the unexpectedness of seeing her come from the direction of the entrance to the hotel.

Her hair was in wild disarray, ungroomed.

Her face was devoid of makeup, pale and shiny.

There was a grim line to her mouth, unhappy, strained.

The shadows he'd noticed under her eyes were more pronounced.

She wore exactly the same clothes she had worn yesterday.

The conclusion was obvious. She had stayed out all night and was just now returning to the hotel. Which was odd. Why take a room if she intended staying overnight with her family?

The elevator doors opened, and she disappeared from Michael's view.

"What's wrong?" Evan asked.

"Nothing." He shrugged and smiled. "Thought I saw someone I knew."

He moved off to the smorgasbord, cogitating on Lauren's actions. It must have been an impulsive decision to sleep at her mother's home. Otherwise she would have taken makeup and a change of clothes with her. She had looked tired yesterday. Tired and stressed. The blame for that probably rested with him.

Had she discussed him with her mother? If so, had she listened to advice that was positive or negative towards him? Pondering unknowns didn't help. Today would tell him where he stood with her. He thought he'd made some headway in correcting her view of him in the taxi last night, but...

He remembered her clenched hands, the nail marks on her palms, the odd action of spreading her fingers and staring at them. He wished he could have seen what was going through her mind right then. The result had been closing him out again and no chance to recover what ground he'd made.

He cut himself a slice of King Island Brie, picked up a couple of crackers and returned to the table, fighting a sudden wave of depression with gritty determination. Whatever Lauren's baggage was from her relationships with other men, it wasn't going to apply to him. Somehow he'd make her see that.

"I am replete," Evan declared, having polished off his toast. "Do you want me to make myself scarce if Lauren comes down?"

"I doubt she will."

Evan grimaced. "Tasha and I thought you and Lauren had something really special going. Roxanne sure must have done a good slander job on you."

He'd done himself more damage than his ex-wife had, but he preferred not to confess that to Evan. "My fault. I should have told Lauren about her," he said briefly.

"Tricky business," Evan sympathised. "You won't get much chance to do any good today, Michael. We don't even get time for lunch until after the pre-record session at Channel Ten. That's scheduled to finish at three this afternoon." He looked at the cheese. "You should have had a bigger breakfast."

"I can always grab something. You're doing the interviews, not me."

"Well, if you're counting on time alone with Lauren, forget it. If she's not nursemaiding me through the technological wonders of live radio, she's on her mobile phone, checking and re-checking the schedule with producers."

Michael frowned. "Has she got an insecurity complex about her work?"

Evan laughed and shook his head. "It's a real education seeing how the media work. Not much runs exactly to the minute, I can tell you. Something else comes up. Interviews get shuffled around. Lauren juggles things all day, shifting, compromising, doing deals. And keeps her temper, despite the frustration of hold-ups and changes she can't predict. That woman has the patience and persistence of a saint."

They were admirable qualities. Michael vowed to apply them in his pursuit of Lauren Magee. She liked her job. It deserved respect. It would certainly be self-defeating for him to get in the way of it.

"Thanks for the warning, Evan. I'll keep out of her hair."

Evan grinned. "Great hair."

Michael smiled back. "Great lady."

When Lauren joined them in the foyer at precisely nine-thirty, her appearance was immaculate and stunning. She had teamed a deep wheat-gold ribbed sweater with her black pants-suit, and added a jazzy silk scarf that was pure class. Subtle make-up around her eyes eliminated the shadows and ac-

centuated their vivid blue. Her lovely mouth was a
glistening red, and her hair had obviously been
subjected to a vigorous brushing. While the
gleaming mass of curls and waves retained an un-
tamed look, there were no tangles in sight.

"Good morning." She gave them a bright smile.
Overbright, Michael thought. "How was your
dinner at Maxim's last night?"

"Superb," Evan answered. "Smoked trout,
braised king prawns and a pear tart with caramel
sauce. You should have been with us."

She laughed. "I'm glad you enjoyed yourself,
Evan. Is Tasha all right?"

"Green with envy. She adores epicurean
delights."

"How was your night?" Michael asked.

"Oh, fine! It's always nice to see the family. I
miss not having them around me in Sydney."
Another overbright smile, not reaching her eyes.
"If you're ready, let's get going."

She wasn't really with them, Michael thought.
Something else on her mind. Not him. There was
not the slightest sense of either positive or negative
vibrations flowing towards him. She simply acknowledged and accepted his presence as an ad-
junct to Evan.

She took the front seat of the taxi. "The ABC
Studios at Southbank," she said to the driver. Then
out came her mobile phone, and Lauren Magee was
at work.

The day went precisely as Evan had outlined. At
the ABC Studios he and Lauren disappeared into

special telephone booths that were built to contain only two people. These provided direct live-to-air links for interviews with radio presenters in Adelaide and Hobart. Michael drank coffee in the cafeteria, which overlooked the foyer from the first floor.

Indeed, every floor overlooked the foyer. Michael was reminded of the inside of a prison with rows of walkways running around banks of cells and the connecting flights of stairs, all open to view from the ground floor. It was quite interesting architecture. He had plenty of time to study it in detail.

When Evan and Lauren reappeared, it was in a rush to catch a taxi to the studio of a popular commercial radio station where Evan was to do a half-hour talk-back session. After that, it was a quick return to the ABC for an interview with a regional presenter, followed by another for a Melbourne station. Michael could, at least, listen in to these and comment on them, sharing in what was happening.

They raced from Southbank to South Yarra to the Channel Ten studio for the prerecord of a popular morning show. Evan went straight into make-up. Lauren disappeared to confer with the producer. They gathered in what was designated as the Green Room, where Evan was fitted with a microphone and tested for sound. The call came to go to the set. Michael and Lauren were invited to watch the action from behind the bank of cameras.

By this time Evan was in top form, relaxed, happy, striking up a good rapport with his host, burbling on about his book in a highly entertaining fashion. Michael caught Lauren's eye and grinned, delighted at his friend's performance and automatically wanting to share his warm pleasure. Momentarily off guard, Lauren grinned back, her eyes dancing with his, and Michael felt his heart turn over. The special sense of intimacy between them was acute, if only briefly.

She returned her attention to the set, the grin quickly fading. Michael hoarded the moment, greatly encouraged. Whatever strain she had been under this morning seemed to have eased as the day wore on. She looked pensive, but not stressed. His laid-back attitude had definitely been the right one to adopt.

Evan's segment ended and amidst a happy flow of congratulatory comments, they retired to the Green Room where his microphone was removed. Since they had two hours free before a telephone interview with a Perth radio station, Lauren suggested, with a good-humoured twinkle in her eyes, that they pass the time in a restaurant so that Evan wouldn't die of hunger or thirst.

Below the television studio was a shopping mall, which led to a classy little restaurant facing onto Toorak Road. It was obvious that Lauren was familiar with the place, confidently choosing a table and summoning a waiter for menus and a wine list. It didn't take long for them to decide on their orders. Then they sat back, relaxed and smiling at each other.

"No call from Tasha, so I guess everything's fine with her," Lauren remarked, her eyes on Evan. "Will you be driving home to the Blue Mountains when we land in Sydney tonight?"

"Sure will. I've got my car stashed at Michael's place."

"I could give you a lift home from the airport, Lauren," Michael quickly offered.

She gave him a weighing look, which he held, careful to project no more than the warmth of friendship, yet his body tingled in a thrall of anticipation, his heart felt caught in a vice, and his mind burned with the need for her to open up to him again. *Another chance...* He willed the words at her with all the magnetic power he could muster.

"Thank you, but it's more straightforward if I take a taxi," she said, speaking a truth he could not argue against. It carried the underlying message that she was not ready to be alone with him.

"I presume Global pays for it," he said, shrugging off his disappointment.

"Yes. Part of my travel budget."

The waiter arrived with their drinks, a glass of white wine for Lauren, gin and tonics for Evan and Michael. Lauren lifted her glass in a toast.

"To one of the nicest authors I've ever had to deal with."

Evan chuckled. "Have you had any nasty ones?"

"Mmm...let's say difficult. Some expect too much. It's impossible to drum up media interest if the book subject is perceived as—" she wriggled her fingers "—too deep or downbeat. Sex and controversy are always welcome. So is entertainment.''

"What's been your most memorable experience with an author?'' Michael asked with interest.

She gave him a sharp look, realised he was not implying the kind of sexual encounters he had accused her of yesterday, then smiled reminiscently as she launched into a story about a group of highly eccentric artists whose work had been photographed and displayed in a glossy coffee-table book. They weren't the authors of the book, but it had been decided they would provide colourful publicity for it. Extremely colourful, as it turned out.

Michael and Evan were laughing over one recounted incident when Lauren reached for her glass of wine and froze with her hand still outstretched and empty. The amusement that had lingered on her face was wiped out instantaneously. Her eyes widened, then seemed to dilate with...fear? Shock?

Michael swivelled to see what had caused the reaction. Her gaze was fastened on a man who had apparently just entered the restaurant. He stood near the doorway as he scanned the tables on the other side of the room to where they sat. Michael did a swift assessment. Tall, well-built, expensive suit, early thirties, soap-opera handsome. Glossy black curls added a little-boy appeal.

As his face slowly swung towards them—dark, deeply socketed eyes, strong aquiline nose—Michael was niggled by a sense of recognition. Yet he didn't know the man, had certainly never met him. Perhaps an actor?

Out of the corner of his eye he saw Lauren's out-stretched hand curl convulsively into a fist. Tension vibrated from her. She snatched her hand down, hiding it in her lap. Nails digging into her palm, Michael thought, and was instantly reminded of last night in the taxi. He flicked his gaze to the man, who was now approaching their table, dark eyes glinting derisive triumph at Lauren. A connection clicked in Michael's brain with explosive force.

The man in the blue sports car, peering past Lauren to see who was lucky enough to be with such a gorgeous redhead, idle curiosity, filling in the time until the traffic lights changed... That's what Michael had thought. Two cars stopped adjacent to each other, a chance thing, meaning nothing, merely a speculative bit of imagination.

Wrong!

Big wrong!

The man had the eyes of a snake, and Lauren sat like a mesmerised mouse, letting him come at her.

Every nerve in Michael's body snapped to red alert. His mind spun on all cylinders. Links formed with lightning speed. Lauren's stress, strain, distancing herself from him, withdrawing to some untouchable place... all caused by this man.

A wave of primitive aggression rolled through Michael. Lauren Magee was *his* woman, and he'd fight anyone who tried to hurt her, frighten her, threaten her, distress her in any way whatsoever. If this guy was looking for a confrontation, he'd get it. To Michael he represented one thing with absolute clarity.

The enemy.

CHAPTER TWELVE

"HAVING fun, Lauren?"

Wayne's silky intonation promised the worst kind of trouble. Lauren barely repressed a shiver of apprehension. Her refusal to see or speak to him last night had obviously fuelled his determination to seek her out where she wouldn't have the protection of her family. But she had Michael with her. Michael... Silly, desperate thought. She'd given him no reason to help her.

"I'm on a job, Wayne," she said, striving for an air of calm control to cover the feeling of being hunted, trapped.

"But not exactly working at the present moment," he rejoined smoothly.

"It's a business lunch. And you're intruding," Lauren stated, a touch of belligerence creeping into her voice. Why, why, why did he have to persecute her like this?

"Oh, I don't think your, uh, clients—" he swept an oily smile of appeal at Michael and Evan "—would mind if you joined me at another table for a little private conversation. I'm sure you gentlemen will agree a husband has some rights on his wife's time."

"*I* mind, Wayne," Lauren snapped, infuriated by his glib and condescending way of taking over and frightened that Evan and Michael might swallow the persuasive line. "And you are no longer my husband," she added bitingly.

"Don't be petty, darling," he chided, again turning to her companions and begging their indulgence. "We have some making up to do."

"It's all been said and done," Lauren insisted fiercely.

Wayne sighed in exasperation and shook his head at her as though she was being childishly wilful and difficult. "Don't let's make a public scene of it, Lauren."

He reached down and grasped her left wrist, his fingers bruising in their intent to take and possess, his dark eyes blazing with the promise he would make one hell of a public scene if she didn't give in. "Just come with me now and—"

"Let me go, Wayne," she said, seething, hating his superior strength, hating his slick presentation of himself, refusing to play his game no matter what it cost her in the eyes of others.

Sheer malicious spite underpinned his words as he answered her. "You're embarrassing your clients with your less than civil manner, Lauren."

Heat scorched up her neck and stung her cheeks. He knew where to hurt. Her body first, her career...

"Not at all," Michael broke in, his tone light and easy, eschewing any sense of tension whatsoever. "I'm not the least bit embarrassed. Are you embarrassed, Evan?"

Evan looked startled. "Well, uh..."

"Of course not." Michael grinned at him. "Soaking it all in for your next book, weren't you?"

"Oh, yes." Evan nodded earnestly. "Very interesting situation."

"Quite a masterly piece of sly harassment," Michael remarked, wagging a finger at Wayne. "You do it very well. But you picked the wrong marks with Evan and me. We have a very healthy respect for women's rights."

"Certainly do," Evan said supportively, getting into the swing of the argument.

"Now be a good chap and release Lauren's wrist," Michael added. "She did ask you to let her go. And while you clearly haven't ingested the idea of being a sensitive new age guy, let me assure you that physical force on a woman does you no credit whatsoever."

"Quite so," said Evan gravely. "No gentleman holds a lady against her will."

Lauren sat in a stupor of amazement. She hadn't expected Michael to come to her rescue. She had been an emotional mess all day, barely taking notice of him, continually keeping an eye out for Wayne, deeply oppressed by his having camped in his car outside her mother's home all night.

Her brother had sneaked her out in his car this morning, bringing her to the Como Hotel, but she had known that evasive tactic might not be enough. Wayne had only to listen to the radio, pinpoint Evan as her client and ring in to the station to start trailing her movements.

His fingers tightened around her wrist. He'd found her, all right, and he was not about to let go. He leaned a fist on the table and gave Michael a venomous glare. "This is none of your business," he hissed, aggression emanating from him in blatant intimidation.

"On the contrary. This is our business, and as Lauren pointed out, you're intruding on it," Michael retorted, completely unperturbed by Wayne's manner. "In fact, we'd all appreciate it if you'd retire gracefully. Right now."

"Yes. And take your hand off Lauren," Evan chimed in with beetling disapproval.

"Fat chance! Stay out of my way, *gentlemen*," Wayne jeered at them, then yanked Lauren out of her chair. "She's coming with me."

It happened so fast, Lauren was robbed of any initiative, either in protesting or resisting. Wayne hauled her towards the doorway to the street in such a powerful surge, her stumbling feet barely kept her upright. She was semiaware of startled patrons looking on in shock, raised voices, chairs tipping, but far more aware of the relentless grip on her wrist, the wild thumping of her heart and the panic screaming through her mind.

Everything seemed to blur. She heard a bellow of pain from Wayne. Her wrist was abruptly freed. She automatically hugged it close to her chest, nursing it protectively as she found her feet, straightened, caught her breath, tried to find her scattered wits. She was shaking uncontrollably.

A comforting arm circled her shoulders, hugging her to warm solidity. "It's okay," Evan soothed as she darted a panicky glance at him. "Best if we back off a bit and let Michael handle this."

Michael! Her eyes belatedly focused on the formidable figure blocking Wayne's route to the door. Gone was any pose of relaxed affability. The man confronting her ex-husband projected an air of lethal power and purpose.

He stood as tall, if not taller than Wayne, and there was a sense of tightly sprung readiness in his stance, suggestive of explosive force on a hair-trigger. His face was subtly altered, all hard planes and angles, any trace of softness eradicated. The silvery eyes gleamed like sharp and polished swords, aimed in direct and deadly challenge at her erstwhile assailant and abductor.

"You broke my arm!" Wayne accused him in bitter outrage.

Lauren flicked a startled glance at him. He was clutching an area close to his shoulder, and the arm hung limply at his side as though it had lost all strength. No wonder he had let her go, she thought, looking at his now flaccid fingers.

"Purely a paralysing blow," Michael answered in cool dismissal.

"Got a black belt in karate," Evan whispered in her ear.

"By all means get it X-rayed, but I think you'll only suffer bruising," Michael went on matter-of-factly. "A just desert for what you did to Lauren's wrist, wouldn't you say?"

"Who the hell do you think you are, butting in to a private affair?" Wayne asked, almost choking in fury.

"Well, I'm beginning to see that my role in life is looking after Lauren whenever she needs or wants looking after." Michael nodded pensively. "I've always had this rather primitive, protective streak in me, and Lauren certainly brings it out. Try to remember that, Wayne, because looking after Lauren has just become my number-one priority."

They had the strangest effect, those words, acting like a sweet magic nectar filtering through Lauren. Her mind turned to a rosy mush. The need to be strong for herself and everyone else melted around the edges. Her steely sense of independence collapsed into soft, filmy femininity, and her heart suddenly felt as though it was floating in a warm sea of security.

"I should have known," Wayne jeered. "You've got the hots for her. That's what you're protecting."

It jolted Lauren out of her thrall of pleasure.

"Why don't you just leave, Wayne, while you've still got a mouthful of teeth?" Michael invited, pointedly waving to the door and stepping aside to facilitate his exit.

"I'm on my way, sucker," came the derisive acquiescence. He swaggered past Michael, then paused at the doorway to cast an insultingly lecherous look over Lauren. "She's a hot little number, all right. Enjoy it while you can, buddy. Tomorrow she'll be giving you the same big chill I got today."

"You're pushing it, Wayne," Michael warned in a steely tone.

"Just doing you a favour, letting you know what to expect." Wayne tossed the words at him in arrogant confidence. "It's a game she plays, turn on, turn off. Easy for her in her job, with you fly-by-night authors providing a convenient turnover."

The torpedoes of Wayne's black jealousy zeroed in on Lauren's heart and sank it. Never any trust for the person she was inside. Wayne had far less justification for painting the same picture Michael had painted of her in his frustration with her rejection. It was pure malevolence. Yet the reinforcement had to be a dead-set killer of any credibility and respect she'd earned with Michael Timberlane.

"Little mistake, Wayne. I'm not an author," he said, but his face had tightened as though the hit had struck home. "I'm more an action man. Keep it in mind."

Lauren felt sick.

"Well, she sure as hell wasn't with you last night, action man," Wayne mocked savagely. "She was in my bed. So remember that when you slide between her sheets tonight and think it's going to last."

On that wantonly destructive note Wayne made his exit.

CHAPTER THIRTEEN

FOR several moments there was a frozen tableau in the restaurant, not a sound or a movement except for the swing of the door that punctuated Wayne's departure. It was as though everyone was holding his or her breath, waiting for what might happen next.

Regardless of her shocked daze, Lauren knew what would happen next. They would all look at her to size up what Wayne had put in their minds. She felt so hopelessly besmirched she wished she could shrivel up and die. She should move, run, hide, but she was bereft of the energy to carry through any purpose. Despite still being on her feet, she was completely knocked out.

"Right!" Michael swung around with a sharp clap of his hands, startling everyone. "That guy is a dangerous nut case. Waiter, lead us to your kitchen. I want a safe place for this much-abused lady until we're sure her attacker is not coming back."

In another blurring burst of action he scooped Lauren out of Evan's supporting hug, off her feet, in his arms and cradled against his chest. "Evan, keep watch for us," he commanded. "Clear a passage, people. Waiter?"

"This way, sir."

With bewildering speed, Lauren found herself whizzed away from the peering curiosity of patrons, carried into a busy commercial kitchen and, amidst the fluttering concern of chefs and kitchen hands, lowered carefully onto a chair that someone quickly supplied.

"Now let me look at your wrist, Lauren," Michael said with quiet authority.

It took her a moment to realise she was still nursing it. Very gently Michael pried it loose from her hold and ran tender fingers over the bruised flesh. She stared at his face, wondering if bad thoughts of her were festering in his mind behind the mask of human concern.

Action man. He was certainly that. She was intensely grateful to him for rescuing her from a horribly humiliating situation. And worse. If Wayne had succeeded in taking her with him . . . Her mind shied from following that train of thought.

What to do now? That was what she had to concentrate on. She tried to control the convulsive tremors that were still attacking her body with embarrassing frequency.

"Could be sprained but it's not broken," Michael assured her, gently laying her hand on her lap. "We'll get an elastic bandage on it as soon as we can, Lauren."

She nodded.

Evan came in. "One of the waiters is on watch, but I think the slimy toad has nicked off."

"I should have landed him on a hard, dry rock to bloat up and die," Michael muttered murderously.

"Oh, I think you put paid to him, Michael," Evan said with cheerful confidence. "He won't want a return bout."

"He really needs that dirty, lying mouth of his smashed in, Evan."

"Better to sue for defamation," Evan advised. "Hits him where it hurts in the pocket, and you don't get charged with assault."

The import of their words seeped through Lauren's daze of despondency. "You didn't . . . you didn't believe him?" she asked on a weak quaver.

Michael's face creased to caring concern as he realised the depth of her distress. "Lauren, honey, when it comes to exes wanting to dig their claws in, that guy beats Roxanne hands down. You think I'd believe *him*?"

"Oh!" Tears welled in her eyes. The shame of having believed Roxanne against him... How could he call her honey? Dear heaven! She never cried, and here she was, out of control, making an exhibition of herself, and the tears wouldn't stop. Her chest was so tight and ... She had to get hold of herself. Had to ...

But it was Michael who took hold of her, lifting her out of the chair and wrapping her in a tight embrace, supporting her in a cocoon of warmth and strength and tenderness as he showed his understanding in soothing words.

"You're safe now. It's over, Lauren. Just let me look after you. Okay?"

"Yes," she said, sobbing. The want, the need to just cave in and wallow in being looked after was overwhelming. Someone fussing over her, caring for her, indulging her, fulfilling all her innermost desires ...

"Your handkerchief, Evan," Michael commanded.

"Here it comes, Lauren."

A wadded cloth was shoved over Michael's shoulder. Lauren snatched it gratefully and tried to mop up, but there seemed to have been a dam burst in her tear glands. There was this awful pressure in her chest.

"Better fetch Lauren's bag," Michael instructed.

"Right you are," Evan agreed and seemed to be back in a trice. "Lauren's room in the hotel is still booked," he informed them. "That's where the five o'clock call from Perth is to come through."

"Fine. I'll take her there. Fix up about the lunch we ordered, will you, Evan?"

"No problem. I'm hungry enough to eat the lot. Might take me up until five minutes to five to get through it all."

"Good man," Michael approved warmly. "Do you feel up to walking with me, Lauren? I'll carry you if your legs are wobbly."

"No. I can walk."

"Big breath, and then we'll set off."

He was treating her like a child, but somehow she didn't mind. She dragged in a big breath and let it slowly shudder out. The pressure in her chest eased. She did more damage control with Evan's handkerchief as Michael tucked her beside him for the walk out of the restaurant.

"We'll go through the mall again. Quickest way to the hotel," he said, holding her close for secure support.

It was also in the opposite direction to the way Wayne had gone. Lauren appreciated this consideration more than the distance factor. Not that she really feared bumping into Wayne again, not with Michael with her, but she'd prefer it not to happen.

Tears welled as they made their way to the back exit of the restaurant, shepherded there by kindly staff. "Sorry I'm such a mess," she mumbled, dabbing at her eyes.

"You've been on overload," Michael said kindly. "It's not surprising you reached breaking point, Lauren."

"But I've always coped."

"First me. Then him. It was too much. Did you get any sleep last night?"

"Not a lot."

"Did he go to your mother's home after seeing you in the taxi?"

She looked up in wet-eyed astonishment. "How did you know?"

He gave her a rueful smile. "Sometimes when I put two and two together, I arrive at the right answer. I spotted you coming in this morning. You looked . . . harassed."

"He stayed parked outside Mum's house. Johnny, one of my younger brothers, had to smuggle me back to the hotel."

So easy now to pour out the words. It was a relief to have Michael's understanding, not to have to bottle it all up inside herself and carry on as though life was perfectly normal. Though at least the mall provided a sense of normality after the traumatic scene in the restaurant. The shoppers passed them by, intent on their business, not seeing anything to capture their interest in Michael's and Lauren's slow traverse of the walkways.

"Did you ever take a restraining order out on Wayne?" Michael softly inquired.

Again he surprised her with his comprehension of her situation. "Yes. But it didn't do any good."

"Hence your move from Melbourne to Sydney."

"He wouldn't let go."

"Possessive and abusive."

"Yes."

"Your family couldn't look after you?"

"My father died a few months after my wedding to Wayne. I'm the eldest in the family. Mum had enough worries, Michael."

"And you didn't want to add to them. You've had it tough, Lauren, going it alone," he said with gentle sympathy.

It triggered more tears. She was turning into a regular waterworks. "Thanks for standing up for me."

"I was glad of the chance to show you I wasn't a total write-off."

She blew her nose, took a couple of deep breaths and realised they were almost through the mall. "I didn't mean to make you feel that, Michael," she said carefully. "I just had other things on my mind today."

"A lot of baggage. Which I added to. Am I forgiven for thinking badly of you?" he asked quietly.

"Well, you obviously don't believe I'm some heartless playgirl any more." She mustered up an ironic smile. "Am I forgiven for thinking badly of you?"

He gave a wry little laugh. "That was definitely my fault."

They emerged from the mall, stepping out onto the open paving in front of the hotel. The afternoon had turned grey, and Lauren remembered that rain was forecast. Pots of cyclamens in the garden boxes provided bright splashes of pinks and purples and reds, but not even their intense colours could dispel the bleak onset of a wintry evening.

The cold Melbourne wind snapped at them. Lauren shivered and huddled closer to Michael as they headed for the entrance to the hotel. Suddenly the warmth and comfort of a trusted friend and confidant took on more intimate dimensions and sensitivities.

Lauren found herself acutely conscious of hips and thighs touching, a heated friction where their bodies bumped and rubbed, Michael's arm slanting across her rib cage, brushing against the underswell of her breasts, holding her to the hard wall of his chest.

The image of his naked body flashed into her mind, the muscular power of it exciting her, pleasuring her, driving her to exult in her femininity, pleasuring him. That one wonderful night of making love together...so very much together...as they were now...or seemed to be. Could she believe in it? Did dreams really come true?

Her heart skipped and started to swing like a hard-beating metronome between caution and desire. Remember Wayne and Roxanne, caution insisted. But they were the past, and why should she let the past shackle her forever? She had a fierce desire to fly free, leave the baggage behind. She wanted to embrace all that could be, should be. Or was that blind faith in a future that wasn't ever truly possible?

Michael was taking her up to her hotel room. Evan was not joining them there until five o'clock. She'd heard them arrange it. Had Michael been thinking...?

No, he wouldn't try to force her, wouldn't do anything she didn't want.

So what did she want?

CHAPTER FOURTEEN

MICHAEL stopped by the concierge's desk. "Miss Magee has an injured wrist. Would you please send someone out for an elastic bandage and a bottle of witch-hazel or whatever else eases bruising? We'll be in Room 404."

"Certainly, Mr. Timberlane."

"On the double, Henry."

"All speed, sir."

It reminded Lauren that Michael was a very wealthy man. "I guess you're used to the best service," she remarked as they proceeded to the elevators.

"I'm known in many places," he answered offhandedly.

"Like what?"

"I do quite a bit of sitting in various boardrooms to get things done for those who don't have the means to cover their needs." He slid her a whimsical smile. "I'm called a friend."

He might share his wealth in many places, but he was a very private man, Lauren decided, not given to splashing it around in public or showing off. It was interesting that he was focused on people in need. She wondered if that was a tradition in his family or a personal choice?

With her acquiescence, he took her room card from her bag and operated the elevator. A few minutes later she was comfortably settled in an armchair in the privacy of her hotel room and Michael was ringing for more service.

"Two of your soup of the day, a basket of French fries and a bottle of your best chardonnay. Room 404. I'll be very appreciative if you get that to us as quickly as possible."

Lauren wondered if those were the code words for a big tip. When Michael took charge, he was certainly master of the situation. Very impressive. He had not only a natural command that people responded to but also a quick eye and mind for effective and efficient organization. Lauren had no doubt he was very highly valued as a friend in all those boardrooms.

Michael Timberlane made things happen.

Lauren mused over this insight as he moved on to fixing her a cup of coffee. For most of today he had taken a passive role, but she realised now he had simply been biding his time for an appropriate opening to pursue what he wanted. It gave Lauren a very warm glow to know that he wanted her so much, fighting for her, looking after her, taking care of everything for her.

Or would he have done it for anyone in need?

Lauren suspected he would have. It was in his nature to stand up and be counted on whatever he felt strongly about. And he didn't give up, either.

He might have acted on pure principle, but his smile, as he brought her a cup of coffee, felt very specifically for her. "You have more colour in your face now."

It wasn't surprising, with some of the thoughts she'd been having. "Thank you, Michael. I don't know what I would have done without you."

The smile turned into a wicked grin. Once again it had a heart-stopping effect on her. "I aim to keep you thinking that, Lauren," he said, his eyes dancing with hers with intimate intent, "because I don't want to do without you."

She stared at him, totally besotted for several moments. *Yes,* she thought decisively, *I want to know more of this man. I want to know everything about this man.* And not on any hearsay this time. All of it would be on direct, personal, first-hand experience, with every chance he offered her.

The door buzzer demanded attention. Michael answered the summons and returned with a packet from a pharmacy. He pulled a chair close to hers and set to work on her bruised wrist.

"Why did you marry Roxanne?"

His gaze flicked up, his eyes scanning hers sharply before lowering again. "I thought we could make a go of it."

"You weren't in love?"

He finished spreading ointment over the tender flesh and started winding on a bandage before he answered. When his reply came it was as though he was choosing his words with care, wanting to give as accurate a picture as he could.

"Roxanne made herself very attractive to me. We were both from a background of wealth, from longstanding families. There was a commonality of understanding on many grounds. I wanted to get married. I wanted a family. She pandered to my interests at the time and led me to believe she cared about the things I cared about."

"But she didn't, really."

He shook his head. "Roxanne wanted me, but she didn't love me. I thought I loved her. I wanted to love her. But as her pretences wore thinner and thinner, I couldn't." He fastened the bandage with a plastic clip, then looked directly into her eyes. No hiding. Clear, soul-piercing truth. "I never felt with her what I've felt with you, Lauren."

It was there, pulsing between them, the memory of all they'd felt that night. And it wasn't a dream. It had been real, special, unique for both of them. They could reach for it again.

The door buzzer announced the arrival of room service. It broke the intense flow of emotion between them. Michael moved to let the waiter in. A table was wheeled into the room and quickly arranged for them, the soup and French fries set out for their convenience, wine uncorked and poured into glasses, chairs placed precisely and a handsome tip paid to speed the waiter's departure.

Michael lifted a plate cover. "Pumpkin soup. Should slide down easily," he encouraged. "Have you eaten anything today?"

"Some toast this morning."

"Try. You need it."

She ate the soup, half a bread roll, a few French fries, and did feel better for it. The chardonnay was perfect for washing it all down and leaving a pleasant aftertaste.

"Had enough food?" Michael inquired.

"Yes, thank you. It was good."

He nodded. "Why did you marry Wayne... what's his name?"

"Boyer."

"Of Charles Boyer fame?"

"Same spelling. Different family."

"He looks like an actor."

"He's done some modelling. That's how I met him. He was used for a book cover. His family owns a string of dry-cleaning shops and laundrettes. He helps manage them for the most part, and that ties him to Melbourne."

"You fell in love?"

She grimaced. "Let's call it blind infatuation, with the emphasis on blind. Wayne can be very charming, very flattering, very ardent. I was a lot younger then and I fell like a ton of bricks. I didn't see what was coming."

"Which was?"

"He wanted an adoring servant. Only his needs counted."

Michael gave her an ironic smile. "Sounds a bit like Roxanne."

"Wayne had four older sisters and a mother who'd spoilt him rotten. I didn't have a chance of making him see differently. He threw tantrums and he was violent whenever he didn't get his own way."

"So I noticed."

"He doesn't like losing, Michael." She heaved a despondent sigh as the feeling of sick fear took hold again. "I don't know what I'm going to do about coming back to Melbourne again. Getting beaten this afternoon will really stir him up. If he starts pestering my family..."

"Don't worry. I'm more than a match for the slimy toad. Didn't I prove that to you this afternoon?" He rose from his chair and stepped around the table to take her uninjured hand in his, pressing gentle reassurance as his eyes burned steady conviction. "I won't let him hurt either you or your family, Lauren."

She stood up, lifting her hands to his chest as she anxiously revealed her experience. "He's so devious and malicious. And a very convincing liar when he's put on the spot. You saw that, Michael."

His eyes glistened with compassion. "It must have taken a lot of courage to set your own course and keep to it."

"More desperation than courage. Though there's really no knowing where or how he'll hit next. There's no sure defence," she cried, the anguish of her fear and frustration echoing through her voice.

"He won't hit again. I'll look after you, Lauren."

"Michael..." She looked helplessly at him. "Even the police couldn't keep him away."

"I have more resources than the police," he said, and once again his face was transformed by the wicked grin that defied the world and rejoiced in a freedom that knew no fear or boundaries.

She shook her head, dazed by his confidence and the sheer blazing brilliance that bathed her in it. She didn't comprehend how he could stop Wayne from pursuing a vindictive vendetta, yet she felt the weight lifting from her heart, and her mind tingled with hope.

"I don't want you to get hurt," she said. A black belt in karate was all very well, but Wayne didn't play fair.

"I promise you, no-one will get hurt." He stroked her cheek in a soothing caress. His eyes compelled her to believe him. "I learnt how to look after myself a long time ago. I *can* look after you, Lauren. And I shall."

"I . . . I don't know what to say." A brittle laugh burst from her throat. "I'm the one who's always done the looking after. It's . . ."

He pressed a soft, silencing finger to her lips. "It's your turn. Let the fear go, Lauren. Trust me."

"Yes," she whispered, wanting to.

His eyes simmered into hers, his silver irises softening to a smoky grey as he tilted her chin and lowered his head. She had the chance to say no if she didn't want his kiss. The truth was she yearned to taste it again, was breathlessly waiting for it.

His lips brushed hers, softly, sweetly, building a sensation that reached deep inside her, coiling itself around her heart, sliding through her stomach in little rivulets of pleasure, tingling down her thighs. Her mouth opened to his enticing warmth and tenderness, the languid caress of his tongue more thrilling than passion. He cared about her. He truly did. And she loved him for it.

The feeling burst from her heart and filled her response to him, her arms sliding around his neck, fingers thrusting through his hair, bringing his mouth more thoroughly, more vibrantly to hers in an explosion of intense excitement and exultation because the magic was there again, richer than before, more powerful, the throbbing pulse of togetherness thrumming wildly through their bodies.

"Lauren." It was a groan of need, his lips still hot and moist on hers as he struggled for breath, for control. "We don't have enough time," he rasped. "Evan's call..."

It pierced the delirium of happiness swimming through her mind. "Sorry."

"I'm sorry, too," he said gruffly, forcing himself to pull back, his eyes stabbing an urgent plea past the passionate daze in hers. "Please listen, darling."

Darling... How wonderful that sounded! "Yes?"

"I need the address where your mother lives."

She didn't understand why but she gave it.

"Now I won't be flying back to Sydney with you, Lauren."

"Oh?"

"I have important and urgent business here."

"I thought you came for Evan."

"Yes. But something came up last night, and—" he smiled ruefully "—Evan doesn't need my protection."

"So you have to stay." She tried to keep the disappointment out of her voice.

"Two days. No more. Then I'll be back in Sydney." His eyes pleaded for her patience with compelling intensity. "Promise me you'll be waiting. That you won't let anything turn you away from me."

That was easy to give. "I promise."

A sigh expelled with force, followed by a smile that encompassed her in a blaze of desire.

The door buzzer heralded Evan's arrival.

"I'll leave you with Evan to do the Perth call, but I'll be back to accompany you to the airport and see you safely onto your flight. Okay?"

"Yes. Thank you, Michael." Her eyes adored him.

"Thank you." Husky happiness.

One last brief kiss, a seal of their promises to each other.

Lauren watched him go to the door to admit Evan. Surely nothing could go wrong between them now. The bond was there, the sharing she'd dreamed of, the understanding, the trust, the sense of belonging.

Yet she could not entirely banish the spectre of Wayne and his potential for evil nastiness. Michael didn't know him as she did. However strongly the cloud with the silver lining beckoned to her, promising an end to the darkness lurking in her background, she knew Wayne could not be dismissed as easily as Roxanne could be.

She could not help being afraid that Michael was underestimating Wayne's capacity to damage and destroy. Underestimating Wayne was dangerous.

CHAPTER FIFTEEN

MICHAEL lounged at ease in the stretch limousine, smiling as he imagined the scene being played out in Wayne Boyer's office. Lauren had a great family. All they had needed was a bit of direction, a bit of organisation, and the heart was certainly there to see her freed from being emotionally and physically victimised by a man who deserved no place in her life.

He almost wished he smoked. A cigar would have added an extra little punch to the image he wanted to imprint on Wayne Boyer's brain. But enough was enough. He'd bought a pinstripe suit he didn't need and other bits and pieces of flashy apparel he'd never wear again. The opal and gold cufflinks were a particularly nice touch. There had been a big spread in last Sunday's newspapers about a lawless gang of ratters raiding the opal fields in Lightning Ridge.

Wayne Boyer was a rat of the worst kind, spreading the disease of fear with his nasty marauding attacks on Lauren. Michael was only too aware of how debilitating fear was. His brother, Peter, had never really recovered from the sadistic practices of their grandmother. That Lauren had managed to keep such a strong sense of self in spite of her ex-husband's abusive tactics was a marvel to Michael.

It was going to give him a lot of satisfaction to give Wayne Boyer a lesson in fear today. Michael could say one thing about his grandmother. She'd left him with some fine examples of how to get a point across with optimum effect. He hoped Wayne would appreciate the thoroughness with which a plan could be carried through.

The door to the dry-cleaning factory opened and out they came, Wayne Boyer accompanied by two burly policemen—or at least what one could call splendid facsimiles of burly policemen. They were, in fact, two well-built amateur actors who had adopted their character roles with relish and wore their costumes particularly well.

Wayne was expostulating vigorously, but his words had no visible effect on Lauren's cousin, Joe Hamish, and his mate, Terry Johnson. They flanked Wayne as they crossed the sidewalk, hedging him in so when Joe opened the back door of the limousine, Wayne really had nowhere to go but into the car.

"What the hell is this?" he demanded. Clearly it was not a police vehicle.

"Get in, Mr. Boyer," Joe said phlegmatically. "We're taking you for a little ride, courtesy of the boss here."

"Who?" He ducked his head to see. "You!"

It was clearly a mind-stunning moment for Wayne—the recognition of the face of his assailant, unexpectedly transposed to a vastly different appearance and coming with the accoutrements of a posh limousine and the evocative title of "the boss."

Seizing the advantage of the element of surprise, Terry wasted no time in bundling the shell-shocked Wayne into the double-seated rear compartment of the limousine. He and Joe climbed in after him, shoving their guest to the end of the seat directly facing Michael. Everyone ignored his cursing and yelling. The back door was closed. Terry tapped the glass partition between them and the chauffeur. The limousine purred off down the road.

"Might as well calm down and behave, Mr. Boyer," Joe advised. "No-one can see in. The windows are tinted."

"This is an abduction," Wayne fiercely accused. "You said I was wanted down at the police station because my ex-wife had signed an official complaint against me."

"He lied," Michael drawled, "just as you lied about Lauren the other day, Wayne."

The black ferocity of Wayne's eyes reminded Michael of a wild animal that had been cornered but not cowed. "My secretary can identify these two cops. Don't think you can get away with any further assault on me."

"I have no intention of harming a hair on your head. Provided I get your cooperation."

"What do you want?" he growled.

"Oh, I thought we'd just talk for a while."

"Who are you, anyway?"

"Many people think of me as a friend, Wayne. One could say I have the reputation of being a friend to quite a lot of powerful people." Michael paused to let that thought linger. "I'm also a friend of the Magee family. And I'm very particularly a friend of your ex-wife."

Wayne snorted derisively. "You can't intimidate me."

"I was thinking more along the lines of exterminating you, Wayne."

That got through his belligerent guard. He swallowed convulsively and tried to hide the flicker of fear in his eyes. His gaze dropped to Michael's flamboyant tie, wandered to the silk handkerchief featured in the top coat pocket of the pinstripe suit and shot across to the door, where Michael's arm occupied the armrest. The opal cufflink earned some sobering study. Michael casually crossed his legs, dangling one obviously Italian shoe for perusal.

"Unfortunately, Lauren said not to hurt you," he went on in a tone of mournful indulgence. "A pity, really. Extermination is such a neatly final solution."

"To what?" Wayne demanded harshly.

"To you bothering her and her family. It has to stop, Wayne. I really won't tolerate any more of it. You upset everyone the other day."

"Tough!" he muttered scornfully.

"Well, I knew words wouldn't be enough to convince you, Wayne, so I thought I'd arrange a little demonstration. That's quite a nice sports car you drive. A Ford Probe, isn't it?''

"Yes, it is." Wary suspicion.

"Cost about fifty thousand?"

"About that."

"Fully insured?"

"Yes."

"That's good. I like to deal with a careful man."

The wind was definitely up Wayne's sails. He looked deeply worried, though true to his bullying form, he continued to bluster. "If you've damaged my car—"

"Now that's what I want to get across to you, Wayne. Damage control. What we need to work out is what price you put on things. Like doing a valuation on your life. You do value your life, don't you, Wayne?"

He looked confused.

"Then there's quality of life. You wouldn't want that messed up with busted kneecaps or other little unfortunate accidents."

"What the hell are you getting at?" Wayne burst out, no longer sure of anything.

"Ah, here we are."

The limousine pulled to a halt alongside a row of vehicles in the car park Wayne habitually used. An electric blue Ford Probe occupied a bay in the row to their right. Wayne had a good view of it.

"As I mentioned, Wayne, a demonstration tends to fix things in a person's mind," Michael said affably. "I might add there is nothing you can do but sit and watch. These doors and windows are power-locked.''

Even as he spoke, a huge caterpillar tractor came trundling into the car park. The Magees had contacts in the earth-moving business. The big cat lined up behind the Probe, lifted its massive front-end excavating bucket and crashed it down on the glistening blue bonnet. There was a squawk of anguish from Wayne. Michael and the two policemen watched impassively as the bucket lifted and descended again, mangling some more bodywork.

"For God's sake! Stop it!'' Wayne cried.

"I want you to stop bothering Lauren and her family,'' Michael said in a tone of sweet reason.

Another thumping, metallic crunch.

"Are you mad?'' Wayne shot at him, visibly cracking up with the destruction of the car.

"The car is only a start, Wayne. I can think of lots of other things to damage,'' Michael said carelessly.

"You guys are cops!'' Wayne yelled at Terry and Joe. "Are you going to let him get away with this?''

"We're not cops,'' Joe said with a shrug.

"I didn't want the boys coming the heavy with you, Wayne. It was a smoother operation to have your cooperation in leaving your office,'' Michael explained.

Wayne muttered a few expletives under his breath as he jerked his gaze to the electric blue wreck. "My car...'' He choked.

"I feel the same way about Lauren,'' Michael said earnestly. "When you hurt her the other day and said such nasty things about her . . ." He shook his head. "I would like to come to some agreement with you, Wayne. It's a matter of damage control, you see. I can do this to your car, trash your apartment, set fire to your laundrettes, make your life generally unpleasant . . ."

Wayne stared at him in horror.

"But if you stay right away from Lauren and her family and swear never to come near them again—"

"I swear. I swear," he repeated hoarsely.

"But have you really got the message, Wayne? I need conviction here." Michael glanced out the window. "Ah, the clean-up crew. I have a very tidy mind, Wayne. I like to get everything cleaned up to my satisfaction."

The big machinery moved out and a tow truck moved in, courtesy of one of Lauren's uncles. Wayne's olive skin had turned sallow. He watched the wrecked Probe being towed away with glazed eyes. A pickup truck arrived. Men in overalls alighted and swept up the broken glass and bits of metal with big industrial brooms. Lauren's brothers were very thorough.

"Well, there goes the evidence," Michael said cheerfully. "What do you say, Wayne? Are you convinced it's a good idea to leave Lauren and her family alone?"

"Yes. She's not worth it," he said dully.

"I'm relieved to hear you think that, Wayne. On the other hand, Lauren and her well-being and happiness are worth a lot to me. Matter of fact, I paid fifty thousand dollars for the car you've just seen destroyed.''

"You? But...but it was my car!'' Wayne croaked, his eyes almost rolling in helpless shock and distress.

"No. Your car is being driven back into place right now.''

Wayne stared disbelievingly as another electric blue Probe was parked in the cleanly swept bay. "I don't understand,'' he mumbled.

"It was a demonstration, Wayne. Lauren said I wasn't to hurt you, but I've always been an action man. It's my nature, taking action. Lauren tied my hands this time, but I did want you to see what I can do. Anytime I like.''

"You spent fifty thousand—'' He looked at Michael with the full realisation he was face to face with a ruthless fanatic. It scared him witless.

"Let's call it an initial outlay. If there's a next time I won't feel so generous.'' Michael looked inquiringly at Terry and Joe. "What's the going rate for a good hit man, boys?''

"Eight thousand is the word,'' Joe answered.

"Yeah, eight's the top,'' Terry agreed.

"Could have hired six hit men for fifty grand,'' Michael mused. He wagged a finger at Wayne. "You're a lucky guy. If Lauren didn't have such a soft heart...''

"Look!'' Wayne leaned forward, hands outstretched in desperate appeal. "I swear she's as free as a bird, as far as I'm concerned. I'm out of her life for good. Okay? Please?''

"Well, we'll just drive around while I think about that. Would you tap the chauffeur, please, Terry?"

Michael lolled back in his seat, watching Wayne through meanly narrowed eyes as the limousine rolled towards the exit of the car park. Beads of perspiration broke out on Wayne's skin. He looked every bit as sick as Lauren had in the restaurant kitchen. Michael was satisfied that at least some justice had been done.

"You think he means it, boys?" he asked Joe and Terry.

"He'd be a damned fool if he doesn't," Terry grunted.

"I wouldn't waste another car on him," Joe said contemptuously.

"Oh, I don't intend to, Joe. I never give repeat lessons," Michael stated decisively. "If someone's too dumb to learn—"

"I swear I've got the message," Wayne cried, unable to bear the tension of not knowing his fate.

"I guess I'm going to have to take his word for it. Lauren doesn't want me to hurt him. Tap the chauffeur to stop, Terry."

The limousine drew to a halt.

"Well, Wayne, this is goodbye." Michael opened the door on his side. "I'd go while the going's good, if I were you."

He scuttled out and ran.

Michael closed the door and grinned at his companions. "Thanks a lot, guys. I reckon we did it."

They broke into wild, rollicking laughter.

Michael leaned over and slid open the glass partition. "To the airport," he instructed. "I've got a very important date with the lady of my life."

CHAPTER SIXTEEN

Two pink lines appeared.

Lauren's heart sank. There was no refuting that evidence. The test results were quite specific. Two pink lines meant she was positively pregnant.

If only she'd stayed on the pill! Her mother had always warned her, don't trust a man to protect you from pregnancy. Although Michael had used condoms. She had even helped him with one during that long, lustful night together. She looked at her long fingernails. Maybe it was her fault.

Well, it was done now, she thought, heaving a sigh to relieve the constriction in her chest. She hadn't even considered such a possibility until yesterday, when she'd noticed a tight tenderness in her breasts. Then she remembered her mother saying it was the first sign.

Having been through nine pregnancies, her mother had considerable experience and knowledge of the condition. Even so, Lauren hadn't really believed this was an infallible sign. The test she'd bought was more a peace-of-mind measure. She now had no peace of mind at all!

So, where to go from here? she asked herself as she went through the motions of getting ready for work. Michael would be back today. He wanted her to be waiting for him. But with this news? It was so... unplanned, premature, mind-boggling.

It had to be faced, of course, but Lauren decided she needed some breathing space first. Becoming a parent was a big responsibility. Her job would certainly be affected, as well as a lot of other things. One little baby represented change on a huge scale. Lauren wasn't sure yet how she felt about it. Once she got over the shock of the idea... Well, she'd face it properly then.

She arrived at work in a state of distraction.

"Hi, Lauren!" Sue Carroll, the receptionist, gave her a cheery wave. "Got anything planned for the weekend?"

"Weekend?" she echoed, not connecting anything much together.

"It is Friday today," Sue informed her dryly.

Thank heaven for that, Lauren thought. "Yes. Big weekend," she replied. Michael... baby...

Sue prattled on about her plans until Lauren escaped into an elevator.

Graham Parker caught her on her way to her office. "The rain in Spain falls mainly on the plain," he intoned.

"What?" Lauren looked blankly at him.

"You're late. Roxanne has limped forth. Your ear is about to catch a drumming."

"Oh! Thanks, Graham."

Lauren tried to do some mental girding. Roxanne seemed totally superfluous to the issues that were running around in her head, but Michael's ex-wife could not be discourteously dismissed. They still had to work together.

Nevertheless, since Roxanne had been off work for the past one and a half weeks, there was something definitely perverse about her returning on a Friday. Most people would have waited until after the weekend. It wasn't as though Roxanne was critically needed in her department. She liked the intellectual eclat she perceived in the image of having a job in publishing, but she wasn't exactly a workaholic.

Something had to be eating at her, and Lauren suspected that something was Michael. Roxanne couldn't bear not knowing if her telephone call had borne the fruit that would taste sweet to her. If that were the case, Lauren was about to give Roxanne a dose of sour grapes.

Her office was blessedly empty when Lauren entered it. No-one actually had any right to be there without her permission or direction. Roxanne didn't always respect these little niceties, but apparently she had this morning. Lauren had time to go through her usual routine of checking incoming faxes before the rain descended.

"May I come in?"

Lauren affected surprise. "Roxanne! How's the ankle?"

"Still rather weak." She hobbled in and collapsed gracefully into the chair on the other side of Lauren's desk. "It was up like a balloon for days. So painful!"

"Yes. I've heard a sprain is often worse than a break. You should have kept resting it until after the weekend."

A delicate wrinkling of the nose. "I was getting so bored. Godfrey is a dear, but he fusses."

The shine wearing off the honeymoon? Lauren made no comment. She was not about to encourage Roxanne's confidences. As Graham had warned, they would fall anyway. That was as inevitable as the sun going down each day.

Lauren appraised the woman sitting opposite her, trying to see her through a man's eyes. Michael's eyes. She was shorter than Lauren but her figure was in proportion and very shapely, enhanced by the designer clothes she wore. Her pretty china-doll features were ideally framed by the long silky fall of hair that shone like spun gold.

Lauren suspected the colour was not natural, but it was certainly kept beautifully. No dry, strawlike effect from continual dying. No split ends. Glossy perfection at all times. It was hair that invited touching. For a sensualist like Michael, it would be very attractive.

Then there were the green eyes. So green Lauren wondered if Roxanne wore tinted contact lenses. But that was probably being a bit green-eyed herself. Lauren had to concede they were striking eyes. A man could very easily drown in them if they were glowing at him with doting admiration.

Roxanne Kinsey was a highly polished package who would be prized by any man who wanted an ornamental wife. Opening the package was another proposition. All the same, Lauren reminded herself it had taken a while for her to see Roxanne in her true colours. Those big green eyes could be very effective in projecting whatever Roxanne wanted to project.

"I feel really badly about you not knowing who Mikey was," she opened up, her expression eloquently awash with sympathetic concern.

"Not to worry, Roxanne. Michael and I have sorted out that little misunderstanding," Lauren said dismissively.

Roxanne frowned. "You don't mean you intend to go on seeing him?"

"Yes, I do. I happen to like the man. Very much."

Metaphorically, it knocked Roxanne's socks off. She started to her feet, remembered her fragile ankle and subsided in her chair again, green eyes narrowing. "I see," she said coldly. "I thought you'd have better sense, Lauren."

She smiled. "There's a certain zest in living dangerously." Though the consequences weren't so happily zestful at the present moment.

Roxanne managed a careless shrug. "One lives and learns."

"Yes. One does," Lauren agreed.

Roxanne looked askance at her, heaved a sad sigh when Lauren's expression remained impassive, then produced a brilliant smile. "Anyhow, I have some wonderful news, and I wanted you to be the first in the office to know." She leaned forward confidentially, her eyes sparkling with delight as she whispered, "I'm pregnant."

It hit Lauren in the throat, making speech impossible. Her mind stuck on the words, *I am, too.* But she couldn't feel delight, not in the circumstances. She felt quite sick with uncertainties. Even sicker with Roxanne crowing her wonderful news.

"Godfrey is tickled pink," she prattled on. "He fusses over me all the time."

Michael wants a family. He said he'd look after me.

"When I had that fall last week, he was beside himself with worry until the doctor assured him there was no problem. He's so proud that I'm having his baby."

"That's nice. That's great, Roxanne." Lauren forced the words out, trying to have some generosity of spirit. It wasn't the other woman's fault she was feeling so vulnerable about the future.

Roxanne heaved a happy sigh and leaned back in her chair, settling comfortably. "Yes, it is great. I've always wanted children. I just couldn't risk having them with Mikey."

That jolted Lauren into asking, "Why not?"

Roxanne rolled her eyes. "Madness runs in the Timberlane family."

Lauren stared at her, inwardly rejecting the statement, yet uncomfortably aware she knew next to nothing about Michael's family history. "If that's the case, Roxanne, I'm amazed you married into it," she remarked as lightly as she could.

"Oh, everyone said Mikey was all right. He administers the estate and on the surface he seems fine." She lowered her voice ominously. "You don't find out about his dark side until you live with him."

Was this malicious spite? Lauren wondered. "Everyone has a dark side, Roxanne," she said sceptically.

Roxanne gave her a pitying look. "Of course, coming from Melbourne as you do, you can't possibly know the family background."

Lauren leaned back in her chair, crossed her legs and waved a casual invitation. "Go ahead and spit it out, Roxanne. You're obviously dying to."

"It's for your own good, Lauren."

"Naturally." Do-gooders always said that before grinding their own axes.

"The Timberlanes were well-known for being extremely eccentric. Most of them died young and in extraordinary or mysterious circumstances. Like Mikey's parents. They disappeared in Africa."

"The Dark Continent just swallowed them up, did it?"

"Nobody ever found out. They certainly never came back, and Mikey and Pete were only little kids then."

"Pete?"

"Mikey's younger brother. He's a wastrel, frittering away his inheritance in Monaco."

Lauren recalled Michael's mention of a brother in Monaco.

"They were left to the dubious mercies of their mad grandmother. She lived in a massive stone mansion at Hunter's Hill and she used to lock the boys in the cellar if they were naughty. It drove Pete crazy."

"Not Michael?"

"He kept a stash of books down there. She found out about it one day and made a bonfire of them to teach him he couldn't escape being punished."

"Not much love," Lauren remarked sadly. No riches at all, she thought, remembering what Michael had said.

"He withdraws into himself. You can't reach him when he does that, Lauren. No-one can. He just cuts himself off."

The tactics of a survivor, Lauren thought. She knew all about the need to remove oneself from crushing realities, the strength it took. Michael understood where she had been coming from, she suddenly realised. He obviously had a very personal acquaintance with abuse.

"As I said, the grandmother was mad," Roxanne repeated with relish. "She stayed in that old mansion and never went out. People were summoned to her. The staff nicknamed her 'the duchess'."

"Being autocratic is not necessarily mad," Lauren remarked.

"Huh! She had to pay her staff double wages to keep them. None of them would have put up with her otherwise." Roxanne leaned forward to press home her poison. "And let me tell you, Mikey is

precisely the same kind of autocrat. He can chill
you right through to the bone with those icy eyes."
She illustrated this with a theatrical shudder.

Michael, the judge, Lauren thought, but he did
try to be fair. He listened. Lauren had little quarrel
with the way he had acted in the circumstances presented to him. And he had been magnificent,
standing up against Wayne.

"Blood will tell in the end," Roxanne said darkly.
"I'm glad I didn't have any children by him."

The reiteration of that sentiment stirred Lauren's
blood. "You may very well prefer Godfrey's genes,
Roxanne, but I'd pick Michael above any man I've
ever met to be the father of my child."

Lauren wasn't absolutely sure of that, but
Michael had stood up for her against Wayne, and
she was not going to let his ex-wife's nastiness go
by without standing up for him.

Roxanne's jaw dropped. She collected it again
and snapped, "Haven't you been listening? The
man is a monster."

Mikey the monster. Roxanne's self-serving
fiction. The idea of a taint of madness in his family
was not a comfortable one, but Lauren was not
about to let Roxanne get away with maligning
Michael any more.

"Well, it's been interesting, Roxanne, but I have
a different view of Michael, and I don't want to
hear him slandered by you."

"Slandered!" She looked deeply affronted.

"In fact, he could very well have a defamation
case against you," Lauren went on matter-of-factly.

"I don't think Godfrey would like it if you ended up in court. Michael can be very formidable once he swings into action."

Roxanne stared glassily, as though she was seeing her life pass before her eyes.

Lauren went for the kill. "With his wealth, he wouldn't have to worry about how much a barrister costs or how long the case dragged on. It's a very touchy and dangerous business, damaging a person's reputation, Roxanne, and Michael strikes me as the kind of man who could make a very bad enemy."

"I was only telling you for your own good," Roxanne snapped, recovering as best she could but unable to hide a flicker of fear in her eyes. "Before it's too late," she added defiantly.

"Thank you. But when I need your advice, I'll ask for it. Now, if you'll excuse me, I've got work to do." Lauren uncrossed her legs, dragged her chair toward her desk and gave Roxanne a dismissive smile. "Have a nice day. Oh, and congratulations about the baby."

Roxanne's pouty mouth thinned into quite an ugly line. She flounced out without another word, fuming with frustration. As the door banged shut behind her, Lauren sent Graham Parker a telepathic warning.

Stormy weather on its way!

Her victory over dark forces, however, did not afford Lauren much pleasure. She fiercely wished she had known Michael much longer before falling pregnant to him. Not that she believed he was in any way insane. He was a survivor, like her, but backgrounds and upbringings did have a bearing on how people acted within marriages. Wayne had taught her that.

For her baby's sake, she couldn't afford to rush into any rash decisions, no matter how vulnerable she felt being unmarried and unprotected by a husband. She needed time to think. It was strange how quickly she was beginning to accept the reality of a baby, of it being a real person to care for.

Perhaps it was best not to let Michael know of her condition for a while. Pregnancy seemed to cause too many emotional pressures for clear thinking. Here she was on day one, so to speak, already worrying about a child that hadn't even begun to form.

The morning passed with aching slowness. She wondered how Michael's business in Melbourne was going. By midafternoon she was suffering a bout of intense loneliness. She decided it was a very lonely thing finding out one was pregnant when not surrounded by any loved ones who would feel good about it. She wanted to feel good about it herself, but she didn't.

She wished Michael would call her. She was staring at the telephone, willing him to, when it rang. She snatched up the receiver, giving her name in an eager rush.

"Lauren, it's Evan Daniel."

Disappointment.

"I'm a daddy."

"What?"

"Tasha had the baby this morning. It's a girl. The most beautiful little girl in the world."

Such pride and love! Tears pricked Lauren's eyes. "That's wonderful, Evan. Is Tasha okay?"

"Fine. Everything's fine. I'm with her right now in the maternity ward at Leura Hospital and she's cradling our daughter in her arms and we're both over the moon with happiness."

"Give her my love and best wishes."

"Will do. I wanted to talk to you about the Brisbane tour. I don't know whether I can do it or not. It means leaving—"

There was an altercation at his end of the line, then Tasha's voice. "He'll do it, Lauren. Evan's not thinking straight."

Lauren laughed. "I'll come and visit you this evening. We can talk about it."

It was an impulsive decision, but Lauren immediately warmed to the idea. Maybe seeing Tasha with her baby would settle her own feelings about having one. Besides, they were Michael's friends. She'd like to hear what they said about him as opposed to Roxanne's highly coloured views.

She rang Michael's apartment and got his answering phone. The message she left on it told him where she would be if he wanted to contact her when he arrived home. Going up to Leura in the Blue Mountains wasn't exactly waiting for him, but she needed activity, needed someone to talk to, needed sympathetic people who knew both of them.

Evan and Tasha would help. Maybe their baby would help. To Lauren, at this time of upheaval in her life, they suddenly represented a substitute family for the family she couldn't go home to in Melbourne.

CHAPTER SEVENTEEN

BEING three weeks premature, the baby was tiny, still a little crinkled and red-faced, but definitely beautiful, like a rosebud still unfurling. The soft little body, the sweet baby smell, the clutch of miniature fingers... Lauren's heart was caught from the moment Evan laid his daughter in her arms.

"Isn't it lovely she's got Evan's hair?" Tasha said with proud delight.

The brown fuzz was tightly curled. Lauren smiled. "She's very lucky."

"It was so good of you to come all this way to visit. Evan will do the tour, Lauren. He was just overexcited about the baby."

"I can cancel if you'd rather have him with you, Tasha."

"The book is important. We can't lose sight of that." Tasha eyed her besotted husband sternly. "He'll catch the flight to Brisbane on Sunday night and be back here Monday night. We can manage without him for one day."

Lauren grinned. Tasha had her feet more on the ground than Evan at the present moment.

"Michael rang. He's on his way up, too," Evan said happily. "If you'd waited a bit longer you needn't have caught a train, Lauren."

"Well, she wasn't to know that," Tasha said sensibly, then gave Lauren a smile of warm pleasure. "I'm so glad you and Michael have made up your differences. He's such a special man."

"Yes. Though I don't really know much about him." She grimaced. "Roxanne gave me another earful today. None of it nice. I remembered what you said about defamation, Evan, and warned her that Michael might sue her for slander if she kept on."

"What was she saying?" Tasha asked, shocked at such nastiness.

Lauren gave them the gist of the conversation, and both of them were outraged at the slur of madness in Michael's family.

"They had too much money for their own good," Tasha declared. "It spoils people. They left their children to nannies and posh private schools and went off and did what they liked. Self-indulgence is not madness."

"And there was nothing mysterious about his parents' deaths," Evan said angrily. "They went on safari in Africa. His father was trampled by a bull elephant that charged him, and his mother succumbed to some tropical virus that killed her before they could get medical help. They lived dangerously and died doing what they wanted to do."

"What about his grandmother?" Lauren asked tentatively.

"Huh!" Evan snorted. "A right old Tartar, she was. Liked to crack the whip. But believe me,

Lauren, there's a lot of people who revel in power in this world. Especially people of great wealth whom no-one can really touch. It goes to their heads. I could tell you about quite a few of them in our Australian history. No-one considered *them* mad.''

''It's true, though, she did abuse Michael and Peter, Evan,'' Tasha said softly. ''She was a cruel, unfeeling woman.''

''She never got the better of Michael,'' Evan argued.

''No, Michael wouldn't let anyone or anything beat him,'' Tasha said knowingly, then sighed. ''But I do feel sorry for him. He's never had the love he deserves.'' She looked hopefully at Lauren. ''We all need love. It doesn't matter how self-sufficient we can be, nothing makes up for not being loved.''

The riches of life, Lauren thought.

''Well, I know someone who's going to be showered with love.'' She smiled at the baby. ''Have you decided on a name for her?''

While Tasha and Evan happily discussed the merits of their preferences, Lauren pondered Tasha's perception of Michael, appreciating the other woman's longer knowledge of him.

While she herself had been lonely in Sydney, she had never known the loneliness that must have been integral to all of Michael's life. His parents had deserted him. His grandmother certainly hadn't loved him. Neither had Roxanne. His brother had chosen to live on the other side of the world.

Lauren wondered about his brother and the aunt in Italy, both apparently alienated from their natural heritage and leaving the responsibility of administering the Timberlane estate to Michael. Was that why Michael was keen on having a family of his own?

She looked at the tiny scrap of humanity cradled in her arms. It embodied so many hopes and dreams for the future. She was suddenly certain that Michael would do his best to give his child—his children—all he had been deprived of himself, the love, the caring and the happiness that came with sharing. If it was within his power, he would make the hopes and dreams come true.

"Michael!" A warm cry of welcome from Tasha.

Lauren glanced up. He was in the doorway to the ward, carrying an exquisite arrangement of pink tulips, but it was the look on his face that arrested her attention. His eyes were on her and the baby, and the hopes and dreams of the inner man were poignantly written there, and in the soft smile lingering on his lips. She had seen him looking forbidding and formidable—the dark side, as Roxanne put it—but this was the face of love, and Lauren's heart leapt in response.

She was holding Tasha's baby.

When she held her own . . . his . . .

"What beautiful flowers!" Tasha said with pleasure.

He dragged his gaze from Lauren and grinned at her. "I figured Evan would supply the roses." There was, indeed, a vase of pink roses on Tasha's bedside table. "Congratulations to both of you."

He kissed Tasha's cheek, shook Evan's hand, admired their newly born daughter, refused to arbitrate over the choice of names, declaring them all lovely, while at every opportunity his eyes told Lauren how beautiful, how desirable, how special she was to him, melting the chill of loneliness she had felt all day.

Tasha's parents arrived, and Lauren gave the baby up to its grandmother. In the flood of family talk that followed, Michael drew Lauren aside, threading his fingers through hers and gripping her hand with the same strong feeling reflected in his eyes.

"I've booked a suite at the Fairmont Resort. It's only ten minutes from here. Will you come with me, Lauren?"

"Yes." No hesitation. She wanted, needed to be with him.

His smile bathed her in warmth. "Shall we leave the happy family?"

She nodded. "We're superfluous now."

But she did feel better for having come, less disturbed about where she might be heading with Michael and more secure about her judgment of him. She knew, as they took their leave, that Tasha and Evan would become her friends, too. They were good people.

Getting into Michael's car reminded her of the sense of setting out on a new, important journey she had felt on the night of Global's launching party. This time it was stronger, sharper. It wasn't just her and Michael's intent on discovering more of each other. A child had been conceived. It added a highly critical element to their relationship.

Should she tell him now?

He settled beside her in the driver's seat, this man who had made love to her more intimately than he knew, his seed becoming part of her, inextricably entwined in a new life. Would he share that life as she wanted him to, not only as a father to their child, but as a true and loving partner to her in every way?

He felt her measuring look and cast an inquiring glance at her as he started the engine. "Is this all right with you, Lauren? If you're not sure..."

"I'm glad you came. It's fine with me, Michael," she assured him. "How did your business go in Melbourne?"

"Oh." He flashed her his wicked grin, then set the car in motion. "Ultimately rewarding, I think. Well worth doing."

"What boards do you sit on?" she asked, wanting something more concrete from him.

"Most of them have to do with funding various charities," he said offhandedly.

"Like what?" she persisted.

"Shelters for street kids. Homeless children. The association for crippled children. Rehabilitation programs. The general aim is to give young people a better chance at life."

"That's certainly worth doing," Lauren said with warm approval.

"It's good when you see the difference that hope can make. Some of them are handed such a raw deal, yet the human spirit is amazingly resilient."

It seemed very apt to Lauren that Michael would actively encourage the will to survive against any odds. More than survive. To move forward and forge a brighter future.

"Has the Timberlane family always contributed to charities for the needy?" she asked curiously.

"All charities are for the needy, Lauren," he answered seriously. "These are my special interests. The Timberlanes have always been patrons of the arts, and I keep that up, as well. I'm a friend of the opera and the ballet and so on."

A friend. A friend to many people in many places.

"The arts may not provide food for starving kids, but they do nourish the soul and broaden the mind," he went on. "The tapestry of life would not be as rich without them."

"That's true," she agreed, wondering what had been his favourite books during the dark times of his childhood.

"Roxanne didn't favour what she called my slum charities," he remarked sardonically.

"No social eclat."

"Mmm. What do you think?"

"Whenever you want to drum up media interest to get something accomplished for those kids, I'm your woman."

His smile held private satisfaction, as though she had confirmed his expectations of her. Lauren smiled, too. Michael had confirmed her reading of his character. He followed in no-one's footsteps. He made his own decisions and acted on them.

They arrived at the Fairmont Resort, which overlooked the Jamieson Valley. The reception area was very modern—polished wood floor, leather lounges, high ceilings, staircases leading down to a bar where a huge slate fireplace supplied a welcoming log fire. The evening had turned bitterly cold, and Lauren eyed this source of heat with considerable favour as Michael went through the business of checking in.

Her mobile telephone beeped and she quickly removed it from her handbag to answer the call. Her mother's voice raised a tingle of alarm. Wayne was making more trouble—that was the thought that flew to her mind.

"What's the problem, Mum?" she instantly asked.

"No problem, dear. Quite the contrary. I just wanted to let you know how very impressed I am with your man of action."

"Who?" Lauren was completely bewildered.

Laughter, happy, carefree laughter. "Michael Timberlane. He's absolutely marvellous, Lauren. I'm so delighted you've found someone like him."

"You've met Michael?" Lauren recalled he'd asked for her mother's address, but she'd had so much else weighing on her mind since her return from Melbourne, she hadn't wondered about it.

"Of course, dear. Hasn't he told you what he did?"

"No. What did he do?" she asked warily.

More laughter. "I'll put Johnny on. He can tell it better."

"Hi, Lauren. We're all celebrating down here," her brother crowed excitedly. "You've got a great guy in Michael Timberlane."

"Thank you, Johnny, but I'd like to know why you think that," Lauren said impatiently.

The account of Michael's "business" in Melbourne left her flabbergasted. Roping in her family to pull such an outrageous confidence trick on Wayne was mind-boggling enough, but his personal outlay in stamping home his point to her ex-husband put her value to Michael on an astronomical level.

Fifty thousand dollars for the car that had been written off, the cost of the limousine, the "boss" outfit, the other vehicles, time of men involved... It was so impossibly extravagant, so...caring. Her heart turned over. This then, was what he meant by looking after her.

"So now you're free of that creep, Lauren. You don't have to worry about Wayne any more," her brother finished.

"Thanks, Johnny," she said faintly. "And thank everyone else for me, too. Got to go now. Michael's coming for me."

He'd turned away from the reception desk and was walking towards her, an eager spring in his step, his face alight with anticipation, a man of purpose, a man of action, a man who cared so much for her.

Lauren knew in that moment there could be no holding back from him. He had earned her trust, her respect, her loyalty and her love. The words *too soon* no longer had any meaning. He had given her the gift of freedom from her past. She hoped she had the means in her power to give him the gift of freedom from his past.

CHAPTER EIGHTEEN

‟"WHAT would you like to do first?" Michael asked, leaving the choice to Lauren.

The warm, relaxing atmosphere of the bar and the open fire was forgotten. She held out her hand to him. "Let's go to our suite."

The communication of urgency was silent and swift. Michael didn't question. The need to be alone together was deep and mutual.

Lauren was intensely aware of his hand enfolding hers as they walked down a long corridor. She didn't notice the decor they passed. The focus of her mind was entirely inward, playing through all the dimensions and permutations of one thought. Michael Timberlane might not be his brother's keeper, but she wanted him to be hers.

He unlocked a door and led her into the welcome privacy of their suite, pausing only to operate the lighting system and airconditioning. He drew her into his embrace, and she went eagerly, wanting to join with him again, yearning for the all-encompassing oneness that shut the rest of the world out and wrapped them in an intimacy that belonged only to them.

His mouth was soft and hungry on hers, and while she knew there was no time limitation tonight, the flow of desire was so powerful, she urged

174

him into passion, straining closer, revelling in the explosion of sensation as their mouths tangled in fierce greed for each other.

Still it wasn't enough. The memory of how it had been on that one night of ultimate magic raged through Lauren, demanding more of the same. Her hands plucked at his jacket. He tore it off. She could feel the hectic beating of his heart, the quiver of his flesh under her touch, the questing strength of his arousal, and she knew his desire was as strong as hers.

Yes, her mind sang exultantly as he lifted her long blue sweater and swept it from her arms. Yes, yes, came the feverish refrain as he pushed her skirt over her hips and she wiggled it down to her feet to kick it away, another unwanted barrier gone. She was attacking his shirt buttons when it suddenly occurred to her, with riveting clarity, that this lustful rush was open to terribly destructive interpretations.

Her fingers faltered, sensible sanity warring with teeming temptations. They were half-undressed already. Action was more eloquent than words. Naked truth was best. The radiation of his body heat was an irresistible magnet. Being naked had to be right. Nothing hidden.

"Don't stop," he growled, fanning her ear with erotic warmth as his thumbs hooked into her tights and his fingers danced an enticingly sensual rhythm beneath her hip bones.

Impossible to stop now. But she couldn't completely ignore the warning signals pulsing through her fevered brain. She didn't want Michael to get the wrong idea. Only naked truth. "This isn't gratitude," she declared fiercely, tearing at his buttons with driven haste, getting rid of his shirt.

"Nothing like it," he agreed, scooping down her tights and hoisting her up to remove them.

Breathtaking speed. Expert efficiency. Lauren loved it. She hung around his shoulders, panting with excitement. Such manly, broad shoulders, strong enough to carry off anything he set his mind to. Did he realise what she meant about gratitude? Better make it clearer.

"I know what you did about Wayne," she said quickly, adoring him for taking such a daring and dashing initiative, showering his hair and ears with hot, appreciative kisses.

"Don't think about him any more," Michael advised, easing her away from him momentarily so he could whisk off her camisole and bra.

Free to hug him, the delicious delight of squashing her breasts against his beautifully muscled chest, skin against skin. His trousers frustratingly in the way. Other things still to be acknowledged and disposed of.

"You spent a lot of money frightening Wayne off," she reminded him, breathlessly matching him in efficiency at helping to relieve him of his lower garments.

"Made me feel good." His shoes and socks went flying.

Lauren had a vague feeling he hadn't got the point. There were far more urgent points of compelling interest grabbing their attention, and control was slipping away from both of them. Urgent needs frayed the last threads of coherency in her mind. It was a sheer act of will for her to focus on anything other than how utterly magnificent he was.

"I'm not rewarding you, Michael. I want you," she insisted, determined that he understand her position and unable to resist touching him to reinforce her claim.

"And that's the greatest feeling in the world," he assured her, swinging her to the bed.

Flesh against flesh, hot and sleek and sensual. Lauren was hopelessly distracted, luxuriating in the feel of his lean, lithe physique, so powerfully constructed and excitingly responsive to her touch. Deep, drowning kisses, arousal swift and sweet.

"Michael..." His name exploding from her lips, a frantic need to communicate before she lost herself in him, lost the chance to set everything straight between them. "I'm not trying to trap you."

"You think I don't know that?" A wild, primitive glow of triumph in his eyes.

"Roxanne..."

"Malicious spite. Don't listen to her," he mumbled, carelessly dismissive of a past that held no power to reach him in the face of what he had now.

He burned a trail of kisses down her throat, lower, grazing the swell of her tight, tingling breasts. Her body arched instinctively, craving the pleasure of his mouth, the moist heat, the tantalising caress of his tongue, the rhythmic sucking that inundated her with waves of intense sensation.

But at the last moment she couldn't let him ... Couldn't, because the image of a baby burst into her mind and she had to tell him. Her hands clutched his head, forcibly lifting it, making him meet her eyes.

She saw the passion glaze clear to a sharp questioning as he realised something had to be badly wrong for her to stop him. He dragged in deep lungfuls of air, struggling to clamp down on his raging impulses, recognising there was a need that had to be answered before he could go on.

"What is it, Lauren?" His voice was hoarse, straining to respond, to give whatever she required of him.

She had his attention. He was listening. They were naked together, making love. It had to be all right. Yet a frightening sense of vulnerability thickened her throat and scrambled her mind. "You ... I ... We ... It was an accident, Michael."

"It's all right," he soothed, quickly repositioning himself over her and tenderly brushing her hair away from her face. "Tell me what's worrying you."

It was so big, so important. She choked on it. "Roxanne said she wouldn't have a baby with you."

He looked perplexed. She wasn't making sense. Yet, seeing her distress, he tried to answer her.

"The truth is she couldn't, Lauren."

"Couldn't?"

He didn't understand what relevance this had, but again he responded, forcing himself to be patient, to wait until she could give herself to him again. "She's infertile. Quite happily, so don't feel sorry for her. It suits Roxanne just fine. Pregnancy would ruin her precious figure," he added sardonically.

"But..." Incredulity forced her to speak. "She told me she's pregnant to Godfrey."

He shook his head. No flicker of doubt. "I've seen her medical record, Lauren. Roxanne cannot conceive a child. Maybe she's now lying to Godfrey as she once lied to me about wanting to have children."

Or lying to Lauren to put her off Michael. Lying malevolently about madness in his family. The sheer viciousness of Roxanne's spite sickened Lauren. Being married to her must have been as soul-destroying for Michael as her marriage had been to Wayne.

The realisation gave her the courage to say what had to be said. "When we made love before..."

His eyes simmered into hers. "It was perfect. The best night of my life, Lauren. I'm sorry there's been so many other forces coming between us, but I promise you I'll sort them all out."

"I don't know how it happened, Michael."

"It happened because we're right for each other," he insisted with husky fervour. His gaze moved to her mouth and his head began to lower, intent on establishing the rightness again.

"No, I mean..." She took a deep breath and spoke the truth in a rush. "I did a pregnancy test this morning and it was positive."

Shock. Utter stillness as he absorbed the connotations of what she was telling him, his eyes focusing more and more intensely on hers as he sought to read her mind and gauge her feelings. His face reflected a churning of many emotions, a soft tenderness, a jaw-clenching determination, a grimace of regret.

"I should have been with you," he finally said, and she knew intuitively that he felt he'd failed to look after her when she needed him at her side.

"You weren't to know," she softly assured him.

He stroked her cheek with gentle fingertips. "Are you unhappy about it, Lauren?"

His concentration on her stirred uncertainty about his response to having fatherhood thrust upon him and the commitment it involved if they were to share a future. "That depends on you, Michael," she answered simply and directly. "What do you want?"

An irrepressible smile broke across his face. "To marry you this minute and shout to the world that we're going to have a baby."

She looked at him in startled bemusement. "Roxanne hasn't put you off marriage?"

"That wasn't marriage. It was a travesty of what a marriage should be." His eyes blazed with conviction as he added, "What we share is the real thing. You feel that too, Lauren."

"Yes. Yes, I do," she acknowledged, awed that he was so certain.

His grin was a flash of dazzling happiness. "Then it's settled. We get married and work everything out together. Partners and parents."

"Not so fast. I think we should work everything out *before* we get married." But his happiness was infectious, and Lauren couldn't be stern or sensible when her heart was bubbling with joy. He wanted them both, her and the baby, no hesitation at all about a lifelong commitment. She wound her arms around his neck and stretched her body provocatively. "Though I like the togetherness part," she added invitingly.

Wicked delight danced into his eyes. The critical talking was done, and the loving could go on...and on, a long celebration of togetherness that climbed to a crescendo of exquisite ecstasy, binding them blissfully to the fulfilment of their dreams.

CHAPTER NINETEEN

MICHAEL finished negotiating the purchase arrangements with the real estate agent and went in search of Lauren, who had wandered off to take another look at the garden. It gave him a pleasurable sense of achievement to have found the kind of family home that appealed to her. Above all, he wanted her to feel happy in it.

She shouldn't be out in this heat, he thought, feeling the full blaze of the midafternoon February sun as he strode down the path to the landscaped harbour frontage. The baby was due any day now. Lauren should be resting.

His concern eased when he spotted her standing under the shade of a tree. She didn't see him coming. She seemed unaware of anything around her, absorbed in some world of her own. He stopped, reluctant to break her private enthralment, the stillness that captured a beauty so special it caught at his heart. He wanted to drink her in, to record this picture of her in his memory forever.

Her head was slightly lowered, looking down, her lids half-closed, long lashes shading her eyes. Her expression was pensive, a hint of a smile softly curving her lips. The wild mass of her burnished curls was tied from her face, fastened by a leather string at the nape of her neck, keeping the flow of it restricted to a thick tumble down her back.

The loose sundress she wore was mainly white with a pretty print of tiny red carnations and green leaves. The neckline was low, dipping to the swell of her breasts. Her arms were bare, slender, graceful. One hand held a large straw hat, its brim decorated with a long spray of red carnations.

A breeze from the water moulded the fabric of her dress to her belly, revealing how big she was with child. To Michael she looked breathtakingly beautiful, aglow with inner contentment, soft and serene and infinitely seductive—his wife, waiting for the birth of their baby.

He approached quietly, but she sensed him near and turned to smile at him as he moved behind her to slide his arms around her waist and gently hold the weight she carried. Her head tilted onto his shoulder, a long sigh eloquently expressing her pleasure in the embrace.

"All done?" she asked.

"It will probably take six weeks before it's completely settled, but don't worry. I'll take care of everything."

"I know. You always do."

"I love you," he murmured, nuzzling her ear.

"Mmm . . . I'm going to need a lot more loving, Michael. I think I had my third contraction about fifteen minutes ago."

Excitement shot through him. "You mean . . ."

She laughed and turned to slide her hands around his neck, her cornflower blue eyes lit with the same excitement. "Can you handle taking your pregnant wife to hospital?"

"For you I can handle anything," he promised huskily.

Twelve long, nerve-tearing, emotion-laden hours later, Michael had an excruciating awareness that Lauren handled some things better than he did, but he staunchly stood by, pouring out intense waves of love to make up for the pain.

Then, like a miracle, the ordeal was over, and a nurse laid a squalling infant in his arms, and it was his son, his and Lauren's son, a perfect piece of magic that mended everything because Lauren looked at him with tears of joy in her eyes and a smile that made his heart fill up again and overflow with so many emotions he knew he could never forget this moment as long as he lived... Lauren, making this happen for him.

Mary Magee, Lauren's mother, flew to Sydney the next day, bringing with her the well wishes of the family and showering Michael with her pleasure in her new grandchild. So different from his grandmother, he thought, rejoicing in the difference and loving Lauren all the more for drawing him into belonging to a real family.

Tasha and Evan visited, warmly congratulating them. Evan's book had been a best-seller, and he had written a sequel, which Global was to publish for the coming Christmas market. Lauren had pushed for this time slot, and while she now had a full-time assistant to do the legwork of her publicity schedules, she had promised Evan she would personally handle all the media arrangements for him and his new book.

It kept running through Michael's mind—Lauren made things happen. Good things. Wonderful things. Incredible things.

To his utter amazement, Peter took it into his head to fly home to Australia for the first time in years and suddenly turned into a doting uncle—his brother, who had determinedly turned his back on anything related to the family he had been born into.

"I'm going to keep on checking that you bring him up right," Peter warned. "We didn't have much of an example, Michael."

"Lauren did," he answered happily and proudly, though privately pleased that Peter now had someone he could let himself care for. Another miracle.

Peter grinned at Lauren. "I can see how successful she's been at looking after you, big brother. You're a very lucky man. Happiness becomes you."

Looking after him. The insight burst through Michael's mind. It was so true. Lauren filled his heart, fed his soul, gave him the looking after he'd never known before he had met her. She made so many differences to his life.

On top of Peter's unexpected descent on them came Aunt Rose from Italy. Having viewed the new generation, she declared him a Timberlane through and through, the spitting image of one of Michael's great uncles who'd captained a ship that had been lost at sea. She commanded Michael to bring Lauren to Capri in the near future, because she knew just the artist who would do her justice and she ought to be painted at the height of her beauty.

Magic, Michael decided, the special magic of a woman who loved openly and honestly, the woman who had walked into his life one dark night to give him the light of her love, making his life glow with a new and happy purpose—looking after Lauren and the family they made together.

He searched for words to express what she had done for him, but despite all the words he had read in a multitude of books and manuscripts, he could not find any that satisfied him. In the end he simply held her as she nursed their baby son and spoke from the fullness of his heart.

"Thank you, Lauren."

"For him?" she asked.

"Yes. But mostly for you."

She smiled at him, her eyes the blue of summer skies, bathing him with a warmth that reached deeply into his soul. "I love you, Michael."

And that, of course, was the answer to everything.

She loved him.

If you are looking for more titles by

EMMA DARCY

Don't miss these fabulous stories by one of
Harlequin's most renowned authors:

Harlequin Presents®

#11536	AN IMPOSSIBLE DREAM	$2.89	☐
#11555	THE UPSTAIRS LOVER	$2.89	☐
#11570	NO RISKS, NO PRIZES	$2.99	☐
#11579	A VERY STYLISH AFFAIR	$2.99	☐
#11604	THE SHEIKH'S REVENGE	$2.99	☐
#11632	THE SHINING OF LOVE	$2.99	☐
#11659	A WEDDING TO REMEMBER	$2.99 U.S.	☐
		$3.50 CAN.	☐
#11745	THE FATHERHOOD AFFAIR	$3.25 U.S.	☐
		$3.75 CAN.	☐
#11815	MISCHIEF AND MARRIAGE	$3.50 U.S.	☐
		$3.99 CAN.	☐

(limited quantities available on certain titles)

TOTAL AMOUNT	$
POSTAGE & HANDLING	$
($1.00 for one book, 50¢ for each additional)	
APPLICABLE TAXES*	$_____
TOTAL PAYABLE	$_____

(check or money order—please do not send cash)

To order, complete this form and send it, along with a check or money order
for the total above, payable to Harlequin Books, to: In the U.S.: 3010 Walden
Avenue, P.O. Box 9047, Buffalo, NY 14269-9047; In Canada: P.O. Box 613,
Fort Erie, Ontario, L2A 5X3.

Name: _____

Address: _____ City: _____

State/Prov.: _____ Zip/Postal Code: _____

*New York residents remit applicable sales taxes.
 Canadian residents remit applicable GST and provincial taxes.   HEDBACK4

HARLEQUIN®

Look us up on line at: http://www.romance.net

HARLEQUIN PRESENTS®

For your eyes only!

Dear Reader,

re: SWEET SINNER by Diana Hamilton
    Harlequin Presents #1841

Zoe's boss, James, had formed the worst
possible impression of Zoe and branded her a
heartless tramp. Could she ever convince him
that he was *so* wrong?

Yours sincerely,

The Editor at Harlequin Mills & Boon

HARLEQUIN PRESENTS®

PENNY JORDAN

"Penny Jordan pens a formidable read."
—*Romantic Times*

Harlequin brings you the best books by the best authors!

Watch for:
#1839 THE TRUSTING GAME

Christa had learned the hard way that men were not to be trusted. So why should she believe Daniel when he said he could teach her to trust?

Harlequin Presents—the best has just gotten better!
Available in October wherever
Harlequin books are sold.

Look us up on-line at: http://www.romance.net

TAUTH-13

HARLEQUIN PRESENTS®

So who were the Brodeys?

Money, looks, style. The Brodey family
had everything...except love

in

Sally Wentworth's exciting three-part series
TIES OF PASSION

Read Calum Brodey's story in

#1843 CALUM

Harlequin Presents—the best has just
gotten better!

Available in October wherever Harlequin books
are sold.

Look us up on-line at: http://www.romance.net

TOP2

HARLEQUIN PRESENTS®

Love can conquer the deadliest of

The compelling seven-part series by

Charlotte Lamb

Coming next month:

#1840 DARK FEVER
the sin of Lust

Gil Marquez opened up feelings of intense desire in
Bianca that she didn't know she possessed. How could
she want him with such dark intensity, yet be certain
that she was falling in love...?

Available in October wherever
Harlequin books are sold.

Look us up on-line at: http://www.romance.net

SINS5